AF598726

THE LAST BOOK

www.amplifypublishinggroup.com

The Last Book

This is a work of fiction. Names, characters, businesses, places, events, and incidents are either the products of the author's imagination or used in a fictitious manner. Any resemblance to actual persons, living or dead, or actual events is purely coincidental.

©2023 Stephen Cline. All Rights Reserved. No part of this publication may be reproduced, stored in a retrieval system or transmitted in any form by any means electronic, mechanical, or photocopying, recording or otherwise without the permission of the copyright owner.

Cover and logo design: Stephen Cline
Author photo courtesy of Vashon Center for the Arts

For more information, please contact:
Mascot Books, an imprint of Amplify Publishing Group
620 Herndon Parkway, Suite 220
Herndon, VA 20170
info@amplifypublishing.com

Library of Congress Control Number: 2023910598

CPSIA Code: PRV0823A
ISBN-13: 978-1-63755-849-2

Printed in the United States

With deep gratitude to my wife, Nancee, and my sons, Brady and Mychilo, who each gave me the benefit of their ideas and feedback. And to the next generation of family storytellers, my grandchildren, Charlotte and Aspen.

The Last Book

-

Stephen Cline

ONE

It's the last book.

Well, let's not get off on the wrong foot. It's certainly not the *last* book, but that's how I think of it because in this age of digitized words, nano-data storage, voice-recognition boxes, audiovisual-display units, virtual-reality bodysuits, AI, and instant worldwide communication, there's not been much need to manufacture books for a while. So this book I'm talking about—which is who knows how old—is a pretty extraordinary book. It's never the same read twice. Sometimes it's short, sometimes it seems to have almost as many words as the *Oxford English Dictionary*, and sometimes it's largely illustrations with only brief captions. In a way, it's always refreshing itself, always a new thing, and thus always the last book made. I wouldn't, however, use the word *magic* to describe it; that worn pebble of a word no longer carries mystery and majesty and . . . well . . . magic. *Enigmatic* is a sufficient descriptor for a book in these days when people seldom make books and rarely even pick them up. While the book has apparently had several owners, I presently claim the title of the owner of the Last Book. It's over there on the top shelf of that other rarity: a bookshelf.

Speaking of titles, that, too, is enigmatic. The light's dim in the room at the moment, but from here I can almost read it: *The Seven Stairs to Bliss*, or maybe it's *The Seven Stains of Blood*, or perhaps it reads *The Severn: Rains and Floods*. It's never the same anyway, so it doesn't matter. Frankly, it can be a little scary sometimes . . . not knowing what to expect. I've been avoiding the book for a while. He told me that would happen. In fact, the reason he gave it to me is because the last time he picked it up, it seemed blank or almost blank, like a palimpsest waiting for a new story to be inscribed over the faint remnants of an older tale. It seemed to him like a presentiment of death. But maybe our fears are simply psychological projection, superstition. In today's world of technology, these changes of form the book takes are the merest prestidigitation of bored microchips. It's just that the book, I think, is somehow yesterday's technology.

-

His final experience with the book was clearly not the best of recommendations. He was quick to insist that it was an anomaly, not the rule, for he had loved the book dearly for many years. Sitting there on his workbench, it was a pretty enough thing, the embossed leather oiled by many handlings. It was something one might wish to own for that reason alone. There are still a few wealthy people around these days who have bought faux book spines with which to line faux bookshelves in faux libraries, but the cachet of such ostentation is largely a thing of the past. Not that ostentation itself has been eclipsed, of course, only it takes other forms now. Like an amateur antiquarian, I, myself, have a certain penchant for old books, and perhaps it's true that I enjoy owning them more than reading them, though I hope not. No, I like old *literary* books, as distinguished from those coming from that era just as the publishing industry collapsed, when anyone could—and everyone did—self-publish what they alone deemed a masterpiece. So, ironically, there was for that brief period a flood of silly books. Then the whole stream ran dry.

I had, he went on, merely to give it a brief perusal before deciding to accept it as a gift. This seemed very like what I would do were I to pull the book off a shelf in a used bookshop—though the adjective *used* has become redundant these days—I'd give it a look and decide if it seemed worth taking home. For a moment, I had before me the image of the old fable by Stevenson about a bottle imp or genie that begins similarly, a deceptive temptation with strings attached. So I hesitated, standing there with it in my hands but not looking at it.

This took place in his atelier, another anachronism in this technological age. He was a repairer of stringed instruments, and his little shop smelled of French polish and ebony sawdust and was neatly crowded with the fret saws and clamps and instruments in varied states of disassembly in woody light that one could easily imagine belonging to a Dickens novel . . . if Dickens were still read today. I was there to get a fret job on an old guitar made in the last century by a premier luthier, back in the days when the guitar was a popular instrument. Now everyone seems to play the light harp, waving their hands airily and pretentiously through colored shafts of light. So I reveal myself to be a bit anachronistic myself: books and guitars. How he stayed in business was a mystery. Low overhead? These kinds of shops used to be common enough years ago. They have—or had—a different ethos, a slower time frame or sense of weight. Like gravity is slightly stronger inside, and so one moves to a more sedate rhythm that allows for conversation to develop across comfortable silences, nudging into small estuaries of thought like a duck drifting along a placid shoreline.

We had been discussing the relative merits of different string configurations and tunings for guitar, cittern, mandolin, lute, and oud, divagating into histories of the instruments and the cultures that developed them and what kinds of roles the music played in those societies: instrumental, ensemble, accompaniment, and the like. It was no mere intellectual exercise, as he had in the shop a variety of each of the instruments. Thus, it was very interesting indeed to hold and strum—awkwardly due to those varied string and tuning configurations—now a lute, now an oud. Words being as ever inadequate to describe sound, I mention only that we listened in an otherwise silent room to strings, sometimes doubled, sometimes alone, of steel, nylon, and even gut, ring and resonate in and beyond their respective wooden boxes. I had nowhere pressing to go, at least nowhere more inviting than this caboose of cultural evolution.

Then he said in that old-fashioned way of his, "I divine that you are a literate man. I speak in the old sense of the word . . . a man well-read and interested in the larger sweep of ideas."

"A dilettante, you mean?" I replied with a smile.

"Ah, yes"—he nodded—"but that, too, in its older sense of intellectual breadth of interest . . . a compliment I'm trying to pay you."

"Oh . . . sorry. Thank you. I . . ."

He waved an old hand through the dust motes to brush away my embarrassment.

"There are not so many of us left . . . dilettantes. The world moves too quickly today for conversations such as this. I thank you for the gift of your time and your thoughts. If I could afford it, I would not charge you for the work on this fine wooden machine," he said, placing his hand on the bridge of my old Goodall guitar. "Alas, I must squeeze every nickel I can from my few customers."

I started to interject, but he went on, and that's how we came eventually to the book and me standing there holding it.

Just then, the door opened—no, there was no little Dickensian bell chiming out—and a strange-looking young man walked in who was apparently *au currant* in costume and hair and was carrying an instrument case. I felt the book gently pulled from my hand, and the old voice said professionally, "So . . . come back in two days and your guitar will be ready to make beautiful music. And you, young man, how may I serve you?"

I walked out of the shop into the busy city.

TWO

I thought about the shopkeeper and the book a lot that evening. Odd that I didn't know either's name. But by the next day, I had decided that I was interested in neither. Who needs an eccentric craftsman and his trick book? Get the guitar fixed, and forget the rest. Besides, I do have a job. It's also somewhat anachronistic, but we do try to make it seem contemporary . . . though our ranks have thinned over the last few decades. English professor. How quaint. Without our old props—the novel, the play, the poem—sans, too, our lecture hall of yore, or for that matter the analytical essay assignment, we have become basic-skills teachers, masters of the short, pithy communication techniques of a technological age in which efficiency of communication is all, and the slowest part of the process is the part inside the human brain. We do not teach sentences such as the preceding one. We have watched and resisted vainly as the old bastions of spelling and syntax rules have fallen one by one to the exigencies of rapid-fire communiqués, the scant skill of light editing of speech-to-text missives. As to logic, well! Some of us cling to the fantasy that we facilitate the opening of students' minds to the great time periods, stories, and philosophies of the past, but mostly we teach them the formulas of becoming proficient worker bees. A cynical view, perhaps, but probably more realistic than the rarefied words found in our department mission statement. There fiction is alive and well.

Surreally, one venerable tradition of academe is yet sacrosanct: the department meeting in which we chew the immortal cud of committee activities, grammatical nuances of "hyperspeak," pseudopedagogical self-evaluations, and esoteric phrasing of reports concocted endlessly by and for administrators and accrediting bodies. Like our classes, these are no longer held face-to-face in meeting rooms . . . at least not real ones. We meet in a virtual environment, a fitting irony inasmuch as we meet to discuss virtual ideas. The savvy attendee can program his projected virtual self, his hyperbolically termed "avatar," to be urbane, interesting, and interested. English professors generally lacking in such impulses of fancy, however, tend to bring their true selves to the meetings. Thus, as for time immemorial, the meetings are dull. And lonely, for we are in reality sitting at home in a virtual-reality getup—over pj's—unshaven, sipping coffee, and doodling with other electronic gizmos. Classes are taught this way too, ever since the great vowel shift–like educational-watershed event: the dissolution of the physical university in favor of the more efficient and forward-thinking—read, cheaper and admittedly, after the devastating pandemic, safer—virtual university.

Our students' avatars are, on the other hand, quite interesting. Untethered to physics or even Homo sapiens' form, they take on whimsical shapes and properties—virtual seraphim. One could wish they would spend half the sapience creating homework assignments as they do creating these alternate identities . . . though in purely didactic terms, the latter could be argued as being more useful preparation for the careers to which they aspire. And luckily the pervasive craze for AI tools subsided when a new generation of young people turned up their noses at "phony tech" in favor of individual creativity and intellectual work. All this, perhaps, explains the gradual erosion of the English Department and curriculum in modern times.

Under the effects of such stimulants, it may not be surprising that by the second day, I had essentially forgotten my appointment with guitar and book. The day passed, and then another, and yes, one more. It was only after a disparaging remark from a student about how boring college must have been back in the days when all they offered were books, lectures, and (shudder) discussion—*Don't forget alcohol and sex!* I thought—I remembered the book and guitar . . . in that order. After turning my virtual sign over to Away, I logged out of the virtual space and got dressed.

The repair shop is not very far from my home, so I chose to walk along the thinly peopled sidewalks. I thought about how easily I had forgotten the archaic feeling in the shop and become immersed once again in mundane life and all its "modernity." As I neared the shop, though, I felt a pleasant expectation, not about my errand, about which I still felt ambivalent, but about entering the mood of the outmoded atelier. I wondered what the world sounded like before the invention of motorized vehicles, planes, factories, and electronic music.

I remembered a hike I had taken some time back with a friend. We had gone into the country to a place he knew of that was not really a designated hiking area, just grazing land in a national forest. We followed a faded truck track across rolling grassland into a scattered forest of very old trees. A cloud drifted in, and as we were quite high in elevation, we were covered by the blanket of mist. The twisting trees grew faint, ebbing color until they looked like spare Japanese ink paintings. The birds, too, drew back into silence, and we stopped and stared. It was utterly quiet. We looked at each other in amazement as if we had never heard real silence before, and perhaps we hadn't, at least in the outside world. As one, we sat on the long grass and fell back supine. The tiniest pinpoints of moisture landed now on forehead, now on wrist, now on lip, and occasionally a breath would stir a branch and two leaves might contact and whisper briefly in the stillness. We were both deeply moved by the magnitude of the natural conspiracy to silence, and under its influence, my friend went straight home and composed an evocative piece for solo cello.

That's what was in my mind as I went through the bell-less door. I was greeted warmly, if with few words, my adjusted guitar was placed into my hands, and the sound of overtones from my first light stroke across the strings resonated like the dust motes in the slanting light from the window. I felt, suddenly, a twinge of pain in the last joint of my left forefinger as I forced it into the tight curve of the C position. The beginnings of arthritis, an alarming signal or warning that my guitar playing would someday, and not so very far off perhaps, come to an end. A presentiment of a kind of death.

All these things, then, jostled in my mind: the silence after the last vibration faded in the room, the silence of the forest, the pain in my finger joint, the disappearance of the book culture, the decline of my profession, even the erosion of literacy itself. And there again in my hand—I cannot now recall the transfer from the guitar—was the smooth leather-covered volume on which was a chased carving of a lute and an open book. I was hooked.

I didn't even open it until I got home and set my classes on autopilot—the teacher these days being more rather than less superfluous.

Then I sat comfortably and opened to the title page. In archaic type it read, *The Immortal Song* by Arial McInnes. There was nothing else either on that page or the next indicating publication date, publisher, or any of the other telltale information that might reveal the provenance of the story, which struck the English professor in me as very irregular. I turned to my console to search for something more revealing . . . and, yes, to put off the actual opening of the story.

I have my virtual search program set up to seem as if I am in an old library with shelves of books. Isn't that the appeal of virtual reality? To create the world we wish exists, be it futuristic or from the idealized past.

I spoke the name of the book and was guided by a little index card that I could feel in my fingers—by virtue of the VR equipment—to an alcove where I scanned the shelves, and lo, there I saw the book. I pulled it out of its virtual shelf and saw a facsimile of the very book on my desk. There was nothing more on its title page. I spoke the name of the author and was led to a reader's encyclopedia, and again, lo, there was Arial McInnes. Next to her name was the terse phrase: author of *The Immortal Song*. Stymied, there was nothing left for me to do but return to the book and turn to the first page.

On this night, after all the intervening time and events, I cannot, of course, recite the story verbatim, but I do have the opening by heart, having flipped straight back to the beginning so many times that evening. The rest I remember in gist—or at least in affect—better than most stories I studied in college. It began:

He was an impoverished young harpist, an apprentice. His master performed for the nobles, but the apprentice did not, for he had one gift, that of music, but the other gift he had not, words. In that day, words and music were married in song and one was rarely seen out of the company of the other. Yet the apprentice had composed a sublime melody, one that in another era might be thought to transcend words, but in his was a spinster. Alone and lonely, he wandered among dusty shelves of forgotten books . . . old bachelors. One came to hand, as such things often happen in such tales, resistant to explanation. Turning at random, he came across the simple lyric:

Lady . . . youth, snowy skin abloom with spring's first roses

Your treasures abound

From sky cast eye to fruited breast and damasked limb

While the sun rides in your hair

Ere long may we not kiss

And be lost as lovers are lost

In timeless embrace?

From here I must summarize. The nobleman's only daughter, as fair as they come, of course, heard the apprentice's music as he sang it with the archaic words and, yes, fell in love with him. And he with her. And given those lyrics, not just platonic love at that. This relationship across the gulf of social station was, when discovered—as they always are—dismaying to the father, and in surprisingly short order he had the apprentice dispatched to a place of rather more exalted harp playing. The daughter, pining, clung to the old book from which the words were drawn, but this, too, her father stripped from her before going even further and seeking out all copies of the book and burning them. But he was not simply a cruel man. He wanted his daughter to be happy within the world he knew. She did not die nor bear the apprentice's child, as one might guess in such a fairy tale. No, she lived long and did eventually marry another and reproduce. But it was said that until her last days, she sang a lovely little song, and she taught it to her children and grandchildren. So when at long last she did pass from the scene, the song lived on . . . down into our very day. An immortal song.

-

Of course, there was a lot more detail, but that's what I remember. All the old familiar tropes of the genre—which are no longer taught, let alone used—were, given my background and romantic proclivities, right up my alley. So I read it again, and again; I don't know how many times.

Finally, though, I closed the book and looked at the cover picture of the harp and book. I had to squint harder and harder because it seemed to be fading. Then it was gone altogether, and suddenly, it was something different. A different picture, a different title, a different story—a different type of story even, an involved suspenseful novel. So I read that one all the way through, too, and had a vague background sense that it was deep night, but it didn't matter because I was in the other world conjured by the story.

When I finished that story, I remember getting up and taking a shower, and in the mist and reverberating heat, I was still seeing and reliving the story. Still seeing it even over a hastily scraped together meal . . . breakfast it could be called, for it was coming on dawn.

And then I went back to the book and read a different story, a sad novel of missed chances and transitory beauty that had a very poignant ending. I remember having tears in my eyes and wanting to reread the ending in hopes that the barely slipping cogs of misunderstood motives would realign that fraction of an inch that would allow them to mesh into the happy ending that was so very close to being possible.

But it was afternoon, and I was sore and hungry and had to go to the bathroom. By the time I tended these bodily needs, the hypnosis of the story had worn off. But I couldn't keep away from the book, and I opened it again and was swept up in a hilarious romp set in some wacky future on a planet that seemed like and unlike ours, peopled by galactic fops and universal wits whose repartee shot meteor-like through allusions to science, math, poetry, philosophy, and bawdy sexuality.

Then it was again night, and my eyes and mouth were dry. My very brain was desiccated, and I went to bed, slipping into a series of convoluted dreams that when I woke, left me exhausted.

In the morning, I got up feeling strange in my house, in my life. Like a heroin addict who with mounting impatience goes through the little ritual of melting his powder in his little bent spoon, I prepared my reading space, snacks, drink, lamp, and pillows just so. And finally, the sigh of injection . . . opening to the first page, knowing that the genius of the book would offer me something I would immediately find engrossing, no matter the genre or style.

Suddenly, that awareness stopped me short, that notion that since the book had never disappointed me with a story I didn't like or some pretentious writing I found off-putting, it never would. I could count on it to deliver a fresh . . . what? Escape? That's when I felt the first twinge of anxiety, but even that was not resolved. Was it anxiety that it would at some point fail? Or that it would never fail . . . it would always transport me, heroin-like, to the perfect altered state of the engaged reader—for me, the ideal consciousness. The page was open before me; the anxiety lifted like a morning fog, and the sun of a new story rose and welcomed me.

It was a longish children's book, something like *The Water Babies*, full of charming and lovely anecdotes threaded loosely along a picaresque framework—one of those stories sure to entrance a child, yet at the same time having undercurrents of adult themes, which at times are unsavory or disturbing . . . at least to modern sensibilities. The metaphors describing various animals or fanciful creatures double or triple into intimations of philosophy or psychology, making the reader feel swayed between entertainment and introspection. Was the author, then, somehow describing me? And if so, I'm not sure I liked the me I saw there. Suspension of disbelief coupled with identification can be a somewhat raw and unnerving experience. When I finished the book, I was relieved. I wasn't disappointed in the way I mentioned earlier; it had been a very good read. I just felt a little turned inside out.

Snapping the book closed, I watched the cover illustration fade, and the vague anxiety I'd felt before returned. I reopened the book. A new title, new story, new world. I snapped it closed again, watching the unexplained picture on the front disappear . . . and with it, a story I would never know. I repeated this process I don't know how many times, squandering story after story, feeling in the sharp slap of the closing covers an ugly power, as if in destroying the stories, I was destroying the drug-like hold the book had begun to have on me.

Opening it one more time, I closely inspected the spine, the stitching, the endpapers, looking for any evidence, any tiny clue that this was just a modern digital creation. Surely such a book would not be so terribly difficult to build by some techno-wizard . . . some bright grad student with a quirky combination of mischief, science, AI, and history. Evidence I could not find. I slipped the book onto the bookshelf, changed clothes, and walked out into the late morning . . . toward the instrument repair shop.

THREE

"Ah, I have been rather expecting you. Come, come in and sit. Let me guess—though it is child's play—it is not about the guitar, your visit. Of course not, unless you accidentally put your knee through it, heaven forfend; no, it is in perfect shape. Immodest of me, I know, ha, but true . . . That crazy book, yes, yes, you're absolutely right—I know—ah, but I am jabbering—so rude—and not even letting you say hello. Forgive an old man his eccentricities, my friend, do. Some refreshment, perhaps? Ah, still before noon, I perceive; would be untoward to begin imbibing alcohol so early in the day, no doubt. And not tea, surely . . . too insipid for . . . well. Coffee, then? Yes? Splendid. A matter of moments, just moments."

He hastened, not toward the rear of the shop where one might imagine a kitchen or coffee pot but to the front door where he flipped over the Open sign, locked the door, and then scurried back past me whispering, "No business anyway, eh." In the rear of the shop was, indeed, a tiny kitchen, and soon the smell of fresh coffee blended interestingly with those I had noticed in the shop before.

Bemused by his uncharacteristic flurry of speech, I still had not spoken a word and then, with surprisingly fabulous coffee on my tongue, found I could only close my eyes. The flavors were so rich and unusual . . . maybe the ebony dust in my nostrils added something. But this was, as I have mentioned, a place where conversation and silence were easy partners. So we sat and sipped among the instruments that shone all the woody hues of grain: rosewood, cherry, spruce, koa, walnut, cocobolo, maple, cedar, mahogany, and the rest. The coffee added one more nuance of brown.

Besides thanking my host for the coffee, I still had not spoken. As I was gearing up for it, casting around for some right way to broach our rather bizarre topic, he began.

"Stories, you see, yes, it's all stories, I feel. Even the music . . . Ah, let me be more plain. We humans, that's what we do, really . . . tell stories. It's what we like, what we respond to. We see friends at work after the weekend and say, 'How was your weekend?' and they tell us a story. We go home and tell our spouses, if such we have, anecdotes, stories, of our day. We dine and regale the table with tales, and then we watch stories on screens, even simple news stories. And then we sleep . . . perchance to dream—ha! Another story there—and those dreams are strange stories . . . and if we can make little sense of them on waking, well, that is not so different from the stories of our lives, yes?"

I smiled. I had no idea where he was heading with all this, but it was charming to sit there and listen.

"So we dilettantes, to use our word of the other day, enjoy the confluence of ideas . . . the music, yes, the instruments as well, but also their stories. That's why we like old instruments. They have stories along with their beautiful, aged woods and rich tones."

I looked at him over the rim of my cup, the steam making him quaver in the amber light. I raised my eyebrows for him to continue, and he did.

"The book, now. No doubt you are bursting with questions. And were answers easy to come by, I would spare you all this seeming prevarication. Inasmuch as they are not, I find I must tell you a story."

He checked my nonverbal acquiescence and proceeded.

It would not be amiss were I to begin, as story convention has it, with *once*. Once there was a girl. Even at the time of this story, which occurred some time ago, she was an old-fashioned girl, dreamy, bookish, a lover of stories. She was rarely so happy as when she could be curled up in some cozy corner with a book or, I should say, within a book... inside the world spun by the alchemy of the author. As you know well enough from your experiences in the university, this was a dying breed, this booklover. And it was not all that long ago. In fact, the decline in publishing books on paper was then already steep, and people with the creative urge were moving on to other media—not unlike the move away from our dear friend, the guitar. Thus, while the girl had read most of the old classics by her teen years, there were precious few new works to be had. She could see, as it were, the writing on the wall and imagined a day when there would be none at all.

However, in a deus ex machina sort of way, the fates stepped in, for the girl had an eccentric uncle, the brother of her mother, both of whom had grown up in an almost preternaturally literate household. As they lived some distance apart, the family visits were few. On one such, her mother, knowing full well her daughter's predilections, importuned her brother to reveal his hobby. Silently, he led them to his study. He stepped into the room and, still holding the door, followed its arc, so he stood out of their view. A large wall faced them, completely covered with small picture frames.

"Is that your collection, Uncle? Those framed pieces of paper?"

He smiled at her and then at his sister and said, "Well, yes, I suppose that's the heart of it, my dear. Look closer."

She walked up to the rows of frames and saw that each contained a sheet of paper with writing on it, some letter-sized, some mere scraps. She began reading them and soon found they all contained some variation of the following sentiment: "Dear Sir, We regret . . . your story . . . not a good fit . . . best of luck . . ."

There were hundreds of them.

"You see," he said in a self-deprecating tone, "I am something of a failed writer of stories."

The girl's mother clicked her tongue and said, "Now, John, you know—"

He held up a hand to stop the phrases he had heard so often before. "Yes, yes, I know, no one is getting published these days. Fiction is dead . . . replaced by some new art. Or as they said of old, the king is dead. Long live the king."

The girl, still staring at the collection of rejection notices in its vastness, said, "How many stories do these represent? I mean, how many times would you send out a story before giving up?"

Uncle John looked at the wall and said simply, "When you write a story you think is good, it should be recognized immediately . . . or else it is not so good. So one each. Yes, each of these represents a separate story."

"But there are hundreds . . ."

"I'm older than I look, my dear."

"But . . . how did you . . . how could you . . . ?"

Again his hands fluttered in front of him. "Endure the unending stream of rejection? Manage facing a new blank sheet of paper?"

She nodded.

"Ah, well, there you perceive the crux of the artistic temperament. Why does the artist make art? For the adulation of the public? Or to somehow try to influence culture with some didacticism hidden in the art? For the money? Or is there something in the old phrase 'art for art's sake'? If that's the case, then there is something inevitable . . . some tragic flaw perhaps"—he glanced at his sister—"yes, some deformity of character that makes him practice his art in spite of the fact that he does it for no one. Selfishly persevering like some mad scientist."

He spread his hands, made a mock bow, and said, "Behold, your mad uncle, the writer."

The girl was deeply shaken by the experience, and she had a notion that her mother was sensible of the impact it had had on her and not a little miffed with herself and her brother for inflicting it on her impressionable daughter. Thus, the rare family visits became ever rarer. But when they did occur, Uncle John had a merry twinkle in his eye when he greeted his niece and said, "Read any good new books lately?" And she would roll her eyes conspiratorially . . . though they never again had anything that might be described as a conversation.

And sometime later, this Uncle John died. His will indicated that his wall of rejection, as he called it, should be destroyed, as it was a terrible legacy to pass on. He did bequeath, though, one leather-bound book . . . to his niece.

The old instrument repairer stopped speaking . . . and seemed, in fact, not to see me at all. I let the images fade in the dim light and then asked quietly, "And the niece?"

He seemed to speak from within a dream, whispering, "My late wife, Marian."

I didn't want to intrude on his reverie but couldn't help it as the half-formed questions started coming out of my mouth. "So it was hers and then yours, but the uncle, Uncle John, where . . . uh . . . or . . . did he somehow . . . what about the . . ."

His voice was soft. "Now you see. Questions aplenty, but answers hard to come by. I know very little more . . . but this has inexplicably tired me. Forgive my rudeness, my friend, but I must go rest. I'll just see you out. Perhaps I will be able in the future to shed a bit more light on the mystery . . . not much, I'm sorry to say."

I walked back home feeling as confused and curious as I had been before. Entering my study, I went over to the place I had left the book. I noticed the room was even messier than when I had departed. And the book was gone.

FOUR

"Oh, Celeste . . ." He leaned his head tiredly against the doorjamb, the shop dark behind him. "I should have anticipated . . . poor thing." He straightened, eyes flickering past mine and made to close the door while I stood on the sidewalk with my palms up in confusion.

"Really, my friend, there is nothing I can do—or tell you. I'm dreadfully sorry that I dragged you into our little drama. Ah, well . . . we should have . . . well, but who could have . . ."

"Wait, don't . . ." I reached out to the door as he began to disappear behind it. "Just tell me who . . . what's happened?"

He looked at me sadly and said as if against his will, "My daughter, Celeste. She grew up with the book but became so obsessed with it—with the mystery. So upset when I wouldn't give it to her . . . wouldn't forgive me. Unhealthy. She wanted nothing more than to figure it out. I tried to teach her that mystery was a gift, but . . . So I kept it from her, to protect her, and then passed it to you, thinking a professor of literature would keep it well . . . but now . . . I must go—there is nothing more to say. I don't even know where she is living. Just let it go, my friend. I am indeed sorry."

The door closed gently. The lock clicked, and I was left standing, looking at my own dismayed reflection in the glass below the painted name of the shop: Lathke Stringed Instrument Fabrication and Repair.

While I was in college, it was still fairly common for students to travel between semesters. I went to Europe with my girlfriend. When it was time for me to return home, she determined to stay on a while longer, though it was no reflection on the state of our relationship, just that freedom of youth and a desire to continue exploring. So before making my way to the airport in Amsterdam, I put her on a train to Paris, where she would stay with friends. It was exactly like an old movie. She was leaning out the window as the train began to move. I was walking along beside on the platform. Gradually, the train outpaced me, and we waved until we could no longer see each other. I knew then as sure as a clairvoyant that things would never be the same between us, and I felt a desolate sense of loss far greater than the temporary separation we were facing. This was very like the feeling I had standing there looking at my reflection. The book and all that it seemed to represent were irretrievably gone.

Alone again, I thought as I walked back down the busy street. I identified with the obsessive Celeste. My own obsessions and tendencies to focus on exclusively solitary activities, from old guitar music to my virtual-reality library, among others, had meant that I had brought alienation into my romantic relationships—alienation for my partner, though unintentional, was real enough. Not that I was a hermit. No, I liked groups and thought of myself as intelligent, gregarious, and charming—at least in turn with my other single pursuits. So I tended to go through serial relationships, intense, passionate . . . and doomed.

-

The world of computers is one of back doors. That is to say that though we, to use their lexicon, interface with the screen or VR image, this occurs at the front, the face of the computer. Behind that display is a nest, a maze of circuitry and connections shuttling electricity back and forth in unimaginably rapid mathematically coded sequences and bouncing around the globe invisibly. Being an English major type, I of course, had no understanding of such complicated machinations behind the scenes of the computer world. But being an English major type, I did know quite a bit about complicated machinations behind the scenes. Thus, I fathomed that there are back doors aplenty in these machines, even if I didn't grasp their actual structures.

Another thing that I must give credit to the technical wizards for is that they have made these machines responsive to our individual perceptions, as with VR, which mimics our projections—my library, for instance. Thus, I knew that I could visualize the pathways out the back door of my computer; I could program them to appear as actual pathways rather than the electronic radio waves that they are in the reality I didn't understand.

Ah, what a long explanation of the little I know. Simply put, I could see by virtue of my VR settings out the back door of my computer, and I could follow the softly glowing footsteps of anyone who came and left that way. Therefore, while I could not trace the coming and going through my house door of the one who stole my book—Celeste, in all likelihood—I could track her movements as she, in the parlance of the cat burglar, cased the joint by hacking into my computer.

But who was Celeste Lathke? That occurred to me as perhaps the most obvious, and least technological, first line of inquiry. The electronic footprints could wait a bit. Already I had imagined myself in literary terms: a book sleuth, clad in deerstalker and cape, peering into the magnifying lens of my computer display. It took little enough investigation to find a dissertation authored by one Celeste Lathke from the University of Irvine—where else? The home of late deconstructionist Derrida! It was titled "The God is Dead, Long Live the God."

Uh oh, I thought. *Arthurian allusions within a postmodern construct . . . or de-construct.*

Ms. Lathke seemed to be developing the theme that we were in a transition period in culture (no revelation there) in which the very gods of the age were being replaced by inferior and dangerous gods (nor there). She defined this notion of "gods of the age" as being the guiding lights, ideas, ethos, muses of the arts and letters, and inspiration of and motivation for technical advances, along with collective attitudes about these. Gods of one era are destroyed by those from the next: the gods of fire and thunder were supplanted by other religious worldviews; the gods of the age of reason were superseded by the romantics and then the industrialists with their machines. And so, too—especially, even—the god of literature was replaced, though She (Celeste's pronoun) had long lived alongside the other gods, tempered their obsessions, and refreshed their offspring. She carried within Her magic mirror of story the insights of imagination, psychology, and philosophy—all of immense cultural importance.

By way of explanation, Celeste went on to imagine a metaphorical representation of the powers and influence of this passing goddess: a book that changed with each reader and reading.

My heart froze. "A zealot, that's what she is. Though I agree with her, I hate agreeing with zealots. The damn book is an icon, a religious talisman for her. I'll never see it again."

I had read enough. Celeste had the book. It was her inspiration—not to mention her family heirloom. And she had built an academic treatise based on an imaginary version of it. Clever enough idea, as no one would believe her if she said it was a real thing. She would be seen as just one more academic charlatan, whereas this way she was as imaginative and insightful as Virginia Woolf and her conjured sister of Shakespeare. As for me, though, if ever there was a red flag of warning, this was it. Trying to retrieve the book would be seen as a declaration of war by the committed Ms. Lathke. Better to return meekly to my classes and noodling on the guitar.

I decided, nevertheless, to read more of her paper (an anachronistic name for it) and found myself still agreeing. She talked about the fact that though traditional literature was still available to be read in digital form on a variety of handheld devices, few people actually did so. It had the reputation of being dusty, of the old-world order, long-winded, and un-hip. The result was, in addition to the "classics" falling from favor, the genre of the novel itself was disappearing. Who wanted to write in a genre that no one would read? Modernity requires speed. So new works were thus increasingly short. Long prose was being eclipsed behind the dust storm of word bursts—which could rarely be more than clever.

It was something of a rant, but she was right. I found myself admiring her for tilting at cultural windmills. Then, however, I looked at the place where the book had lain, and I felt a rush of heat in my chest and face. The woman, whatever her admirable ideas about the state of the novel in modern society, had broken into my home and stolen from me. She could have knocked on the door and presented her claim. A civilized conversation, not this violation.

And then it occurred to me: if no one was writing novels anymore, the book, this "last book," whether mechanical or magical, was essentially the only source left of new, long-prose works. And it seemed inexhaustible. It was, therefore, almost unimaginably valuable, a priceless cultural treasure—not just of the past, but . . . I didn't even know how to put it into words. The book was like some kind of ancient wellspring, gushing fresh, newly made water every minute . . . an expression of the muse . . . a . . . oh, Celeste, damn you . . . the book is a goddess.

—

There was little more information about Celeste Lathke to be found in standard searches. So it was back to the backdoor, my decision to give up sleuthing forgotten. As I mentioned before, programming my computer to show me the electronic footprints around my virtual space in visual form is a matter of a few clicks of virtual buttons. I was surprised, however, at how many footprints there were. I set the system to show the digital tracks within my existing "library" configuration, so I could literally see them among the stacks as glowing footprints of differing colors based on the source of the intrusion. Thus, I could, as it were, walk along the electronic pathway back to the origins, the person, or at least the machine of the person who had probed my system. There were, perhaps, a dozen sets of footprints leading out of my library into the mazelike tunnels of cyberspace. What was this evidence about, this creeping through my library and fingering my treasures?

After a few forays, I realized that most were poorly concealed attempts by students to sneak a peek at my final exams. Much good it would do them. I tenaciously clung to the idea that an exam was a place for students to apply and practice what they learned in the class: to think, organize, and express cogently. Another old-fashioned view. It would give them little advantage to tiptoe around my computer to find an exam that had one question that said something like: Apply three of the methods of analysis we studied in the course to such and such. Discuss in detail. I told them in class that was the test. Dumb. So I wasted a bunch of time tracing down these worthy souls and leaving my official calling card to give them the willies.

That left the faint blue footprints. Faint because the person had tried to erase her passage. It was surely a her . . . Celeste Lathke.

I configured my search program to concentrate bloodhound-like on these faint traces of her coming and going, filtering out the billions of confusing electronic impulses that fired invisibly through the vast network. Thus, I floated through what looked in my VR display like a tapestry of tunnels twisting, merging, crossing, and branching, always following the faint blue glow of her track. A convoluted track it was. It was like the detective stories where someone is being chased through a dense city. He ducks down an alley, into the backdoor of a bustling kitchen, up the stairs to the roof, leaps across to the adjoining roof, down the fire escape, into a passing taxi, disappearing into the sea of cars and people. Celeste's partly obscured tracks mocked her attempts, however. I could see every turn, every switchback. Finally, I came out of the anonymous tunnels into what seemed an old-fashioned entryway into a medieval manor. I paused, then moved forward into the arched passageway and stopped. That is, everything stopped. My display froze, the image pixilated and extinguished. My computer crashed, and I was powerless and blind.

Apparently, Celeste's back door was better protected than mine. I took off my VR headset, tossed it on the desk, and looked stupidly at my stunned computer VR station. Stymied.

FIVE

Our technical ability to talk with virtually anyone on the planet in an instant notwithstanding, we were living in a very personally isolated time. The machines kept most of us at home where we found our work, friends, and pleasures via the intermediary of networked computers. When mine shut down, I was alone in a profound way. It was a claustrophobic sensation. I bolted.

Without premeditation, scarcely without conscious awareness, I followed the sidewalks toward the little repair shop. Surely the old man could tell me where Celeste lived. But when I got near, I saw him fumbling with a key at the door. He was locking it. Then without looking my direction, he hunched into his scarf and scurried away down the sidewalk.

Of course, I followed.

It's not that hard to follow an old, worried man on city sidewalks. I hung well back and eased along. He never looked other than straight ahead except to cross a street when he gave the barest of glances for traffic. It was quite a ways, though, and I wondered why he hadn't taken public transportation. Okay, I was getting tired and wished we could hop on a tram for a while. Tough old bugger. Although he didn't dive down any alleys or through any kitchens, it was a circuitous route into parts of the city I never went, once lightly industrial, then restored into hip gentility and then slipping into decline. Shabbiness was only a generation away.

Mr. Lathke finally stopped at an old brick building that looked like it had once been a factory that had been remodeled sometime back into flats and lofts. I could see through a wide, open entryway to a courtyard garden complete with a splashing fountain. Ground-floor apartments opened onto the courtyard while stairs spiraled up in the corners. Doors were painted in brilliant Dublinesque colors that looked cheery against the old bricks.

I stood at the edge of the entryway looking around the corner, undoubtedly in a manner sure to arouse suspicion should I be seen by a neighbor. Mr. Lathke was standing irresolute next to the fountain, looking at a ground-floor corner apartment, where two young men were just exiting. They were speaking quietly and shaking their heads, as if in consternation. Then they saw Lathke. Everyone—even the fountain!—seemed to freeze into a tableau. They recognized him and, before he could react, bounded up to him and stood face-to-face. One grabbed Lathke's arm above the elbow and whispered something fiercely to him.

He replied in a loud frightened voice, "I don't know where she is. What do you want with her? No, I haven't seen her in weeks! No, believe me!"

After a brief consultation, the men seemed to come to the conclusion that the old man was too frightened to lie, and so began walking rapidly toward the entryway, toward me. I scampered back in surprise and, yes, some fear. Then I affected a casual but purposeful stride along the sidewalk, like someone heading to his nearby home. What had I learned? Celeste was not there. Her father didn't know where she was. Two threatening young men seemed eager to track her down. What should I do? It would be of no value to stop and talk to Mr. Lathke. He would be further dismayed by my presence. He clearly did not know the young men.

My mind was made up for me when the men brushed by me on the sidewalk and I caught a shred of their conversation.

"If she's gone to ground, it'll be a bitch to find her."

"We'll have to search for her electronically from the office."

"That damn book."

Of course, I followed.

It's not that hard to trail a couple of intent young men who have no expectation of being followed. As before, I hung back and eased along, though somewhat more quickly than with the old gentleman. These were not the thugs of noir tales. They were not even particularly athletic. In fact, they looked the type that had spent their fairly recent college years in the bowels of the computer department . . . what an earlier age would have labeled *nerds*. After several turns, however, the similarity to my earlier stalking ended. They hopped into a car and sped away, but not before I read the license plate. My memory is not what it once was, so I repeated the number over and over and over on my long way home.

As it turned out, I needn't have bothered. By the time I got home, it was twilight, that time that used to be called by the poetic term *the gloaming*. Switching on my living room light, I was taken aback—yet somehow unsurprised, if that is possible—to see sitting on my couch a woman I knew immediately as . . . Celeste Lathke.

For people who had come out of the English Department, it took us a long time to get past the staring phase and into spoken language. It seemed as if we had entire conversations—questions, answers, accusations, explanations—in those long seconds that I stood in the doorway with her admittedly rather attractive face tilted up toward me, side lit by the yellowish illumination of the end table lamp.

Truth be told, I didn't know where to start. I walked over to the refrigerator, pulled out an open bottle of Mosel Piesporter, poured two small glasses, placed one at her elbow, and then sat in the overstuffed chair opposite her.

She picked up her wine and took a sip, while I raised my professorial mask and finally said, "I've been thinking, Celeste; in actual fact, your dissertation doesn't go far enough in your conclusions regarding the cultural shift vis-à-vis the reading of novels. Not simply have people been reading *novels* less, they are reading less. Technology has made the use of writing itself less necessary. Writing is a tool of communication, and when new devices made instant communication worldwide possible, there began a decrease in dependence on the written word. It is simply becoming obsolete. Oh, it will probably never disappear, but just as the cultures that used books and written histories supplanted oral cultures in which history and knowledge were transmitted down the generations by word of mouth and memory, now that written-word method of books is being eclipsed by the visual and auditory techniques available through virtual reality and the like—memory being the work, now, of the computer. We are, not to put too fine a point on it, becoming a post-literate society."

"I wrote that a few years ago, but I agree with you. Epochal change may well be happening, and I suppose *post-literate* is an apt descriptor. Mmm . . . this is lovely wine, Professor Sutton . . . or"—irony crept into her tone—"do you prefer the honorific, Doctor?"

"You may as well call me Charles."

"So given that analysis, would you consider yourself as an English professor something like the little Dutch girl trying to hold back the flood with her finger in the hole in the dike?"

"I don't recall the end of that story. Didn't she drown?"

"Everyone who tries to maintain some moral stance drowns . . . sooner or later."

"Then what character would you be? Some great seafarer, no doubt. Or maybe the Lady of the Lake?"

"Oh no, I'll drown too, probably sooner than the little girl."

"Trying to swim upstream in a barrel, it seems. More wine?"

"Please."

While I went through the motions, I examined her more carefully . . . and she me—like diplomats preparing for the potentially contentious negotiations after the obligatory niceties and clever sparring.

Celeste looked like the poster child for the internationalization of the human gene pool. She had clavicle-length, wavy auburn hair over a café au lait face, a straight, thin nose above full lips bracketed by high cheek bones and slightly almond-shaped eyes that were light brown, nearly amber. The latter gave her the faintly feral look of a house cat that might at any moment revert to the wild hunter it conceals behind its inscrutable facade. I had the sense that when she uncoiled from my couch, the cat analogies would continue to suggest themselves. Her claws were, for the nonce, retracted, but given her proclivities for breaking and entering, I was wary of them.

When I settled again in my chair, I said, "As you may imagine, I have quite a few questions about this rather unusual book, as well as the burglary of my home—not to mention the unsavory fellows who . . . visited yours. First, though, why the hell are you here? Why come back? No, wait, how the hell did you know I even had the book? Given what he told me of your family, I can't believe your dad would have told you."

"Okay. Yes, you are right. He didn't tell me in so many words. It was just a timing thing. Good for me . . . bad for you, I guess. I bring him dinner some nights, irregularly. I arrived apparently just after you left. He waxed lyrically about some professor fellow, a fellow dilettante he had connected with. And later he was talking about retiring and all the stuff he would need to deal with. I put two and two together, suspicious girl that I am, and being techie to boot, well, curiosity got the better of me.

"Cruising through your library was pretty interesting in an old-school kind of way. I like the cozy layout, like in a novel. When I came across your circular search about Arial McInnes, I guessed you had the book . . . and I . . . well . . . yeah. You know the rest of that part. As for why I am here now . . . that's a bit harder to rationalize. My dad has had a very scary encounter with those—what did you call them?—'unsavory fellows,' and I really didn't want to myself. I couldn't very well go to the shop where they were likely keeping a watch . . . I just needed a place where I could . . . I don't know . . . think of what to do, or something. I obviously was too shook to consider it very well."

She stood up. "I should go . . ."

"Sit down. If nothing else, I have a lot more questions."

She sat, and we looked at each other, trying to read into what little our faces revealed.

Her eyes tightened; then the unpredictable woman replied, "Tell me about the first story you read in the book. Do you remember what it was about?"

I realized then that we would continue along a circuitous path in this discussion, but having read her work, I knew her to be very intelligent, so I decided to follow her lead. I also had no particular desire to spark the kindling of her zealotry with a display of my anger.

So I told her the story of *The Immortal Song*: the apprentice harper and the nobleman's daughter, their doomed love, his death at the hands of her father, her father's attempt to eradicate the lyrics, and finally of the song she passed down to her children.

During this recital, Celeste had closed her eyes and let her head rest on the soft couch back. Her face lost its feline sharpness and took on rather the appearance of a child. I found myself telling the story to that child like a bedtime story.

When I stopped, she opened her eyes, and twin tears traced identical trails down her cheeks. Her face retained that childlike quality.

She spoke so softly I had to lean forward to hear her. "You are an ally, then, and not an enemy. I have been struggling by myself for so long."

I was beginning to get used to being confused. I waited for her to resume, which eventually she did, her head lifting off the couch.

"It is an important story. Oh, I know you don't know why, but now I can explain some things to you. I was afraid to give you any information that would give you a reason to . . . well, let me back up. The first story is always significant because the book's most amazing property is not that it tells a different story every time."

She raised a single finger for emphasis and, in response to my raised eyebrows and open mouth, said, "Yes, you're right, that is an amazing property, but the most amazing thing is that it tells a different first story to each reader, and this is it, the story is somehow reflective of that individual reader's personality, his or her psychological components, strengths, and weaknesses. And in a strange way, it is a window or guide to that person's greater role in the world."

I had been riveted until this last statement, but this threw me into skepticism. "What, like a tarot card reading or something? That's a bit much to swallow. I mean, come on, it's plenty strange enough just switching stories, but this . . . I don't know what to call it . . ."

"Magic?" she said softly.

I sat still and looked at her closely. Was this woman crazy? Her face was still as guileless as a maiden. She let me look deeply into unguarded eyes.

Then she asked, "Are you able to believe in magic? As a professor of literature, can you at least suspend disbelief for the course of a story, for the course of this story?"

"This story?"

"Of course. What did you think this was? The random happenstance of post-modern existence?"

She was smiling now, and I began to join her but suddenly sprang from my chair, shaking off the seduction of the mysterious the way one closes a murder mystery after reading too many hours in a row.

I retreated again to the kitchen, muttering, "We better eat something. My blood sugar is way too low for this stuff with wine."

I began going through the calming steps of preparing chicken piccata, never asking my "guest" if she liked it or wanted some or even if she was staying. I sensed only that she was watching me as I sliced onions and garlic and squeezed lemon juice. At one point, I turned with the knife slightly raised and said, "I haven't forgotten those geek thugs that seemed to be after you . . . but not now. Now is for food," and I returned to my cooking while she sat still and silent on the couch.

While I was breading the chicken, I looked up and saw that Celeste was stretched out on the couch, apparently sound asleep. It was a pretty good place to stall dinner, so I stopped what I was doing and sat at the kitchen table. I began thinking about what she had said, not so much the magic stuff but about being a literature professor. I had not applied literary analysis to any of this and, being a believer that such thinking should not be restricted to the academy, sought to do so now.

What about that first story, *The Immortal Song*? What was that really about thematically? The carrying on of some romantic theme, communicating it freshly to a new generation, perhaps. What about in terms of Bakhtinian analysis in which the arts are considered dialogic, that is, conversational, one artist learning from earlier artists and responding to or reacting against their works so there is this back-and-forth evolution?

In this case, first, really, would be the lyrics from the old book that the harpist had found. He added his music to it, changing it for his era, building on the expression of the theme by adding music to the romantic words. Then on his death, the lady sent it on to her progeny as an a cappella song for children. One wonders how they would respond, being inexperienced lovers. But isn't it often like that? The children learning of love—and sex—through such folkloric means? Now, taking all that as the life of the theme, its reality, we would have to add the story I read in the book as a further incarnation of the artistic theme in this present era. And then my oral recitation of it to Celeste . . .

Okay, now the big picture. Step back and contextualize, draw parallels, look for universal applications. The story is as much about the preservation or the protection of the romantic theme as the development of song itself. The theme is threatened with extinction by the lady's father—with book burnings and such—yet she finds a way to safeguard it, sending it on into the future. Saving the art from the pragmatic king who has no place in his worldview for such airy arts. And what do we see? The Last Book, and Celeste trying to save it from whatever threat that now seems to hang over it. And this is directly linked to both our analyses of the state of literature in culture and our commitments to keeping it alive—even my weak attempts to incorporate it in my composition courses. The king of our culture has no interest in this art form. Celeste was right about the muses.

I was lost enough in this thought process that I noticed nothing until she sat down across from me. Catlike in her movements, yes, but tall for a cat.

"I thought you were hungry."

"Yes, well, when you fell asleep, I thought I'd wait and let you rest. The food can keep. You hungry now?"

"Ravenous."

“Are you a carnivore? I’m making chicken piccata.”

“Sounds delicious. Can I help?”

“No, all the work’s basically done.”

I rose to return to the food preparation. As I passed her, she touched my arm and looked at me with a vulnerability I’d not seen and said, “Professor, I mean . . . Charles . . . you have been very kind. I know this has been, well”—she smiled awkwardly—“an unusual set of circumstances . . . I mean, I broke into your home—twice now—and there’s this weird book and these guys chasing me . . . and you haven’t called the cops . . . or the men in the white coats.”

“Don’t forget making you dinner,” I replied, suddenly wanting to deflect her sincerity.

She seemed instantly to understand and laughed and said, “And plying me with wine and poetry. Classic professorial seduction.”

I smiled down at her and said, “Let’s not get ahead of ourselves. I’m actually thinking about poisoning you for that book.”

Something seemed to flicker in her eyes for the briefest second, and then she laughed. I thought, *Okay, back to our places across the chessboard. Friendly, but not yet friends.*

Dinner was very good, and our conversation was quite sparse. It was like we were off duty, simply comfortable and enjoying the flavors. She remarked on how the herbs and garlic brought out a new spiciness in the wine we finished off. And I talked about the local farmers market. That kind of conversation.

Afterward, Celeste insisted on doing the cleanup as her contribution. I let her, though I wouldn’t allow most guests to do so. I watched her and saw in her actions the competency of much practice, a self-reliance that hinted at a solitary life. When she was finished, she turned and leaned against the sink, drying her hands, looking satisfied with a simple job that offered immediate rewards.

Then, as if turning a corner in her mind, she asked, "What were you thinking about so seriously while I was sleeping?"

"Oh, ponderous, academic analysis. I'm too stuffed to recapitulate it all now."

She came back to the table and turned a chair around and sat down with her arms crossed over the back. "Tell me."

"Oh please, it's, you know, lit crit. I'd bore you."

"You're forgetting, that's my field too. Out with it, Professor."

So I went over the thematic and Bakhtinian analyses I had considered before, and in true English-professor style, instead of giving a brief synopsis, I expounded in quite some depth, warming to the topic again and spinning out further permutations with apposite divagations to an apparently rapt audience. When I finished, I felt a bit embarrassed.

"Sorry, didn't mean to show off. I get carried away sometimes. The old teacher-centered pedagogy kicks in and I go off on an old-fashioned lecture."

"I miss lectures. Group work sucks. Students need to hear smart people talk sometimes. And thank you for the analysis. I'm feeling better about all this. You know we do have some commonalities."

I thought about that for a moment and then said, "Tell me about your first story from the book."

To my surprise, the pleasure on her face fell away, and she looked at me strangely. Then one-half of her mouth pulled up into a weak half smile, and she said, "Okay. You're right to ask. My turn . . . only . . . well, you'll see."

"Do you want to move back into the living room?"

"Too dark. Let's stay here."

"Okay."

"I was quite young when I read my first story. It was my mother's book then, and she was secretive about it. I saw her deeply engrossed in it, but when faced with my childish questions and requests to be read a story, she laughed and said the book was not for little girls and put it away on a shelf I couldn't reach. But of course, one day I did reach it by way of a very strong curiosity and a tall chair. Mother was busy elsewhere in the house, and so I sat right down on the chair and opened the book. It was obviously a children's book, a fairy tale. Russian, I know now, with delicate and detailed color drawings as illustrations.

"It was about a little peasant girl living in a forest with her poor family. She received a simple wooden doll as a gift. She loved the doll and kept it with her always. After a long time, she noticed a line, like a crack around the middle. She worried over it and fiddled with it until it widened and eventually the doll broke in half. She was mortified but then surprised to find another smaller doll inside. It was one of those nesting dolls . . . but she'd no idea. Before long, she had opened many, each smaller than the next, a perfect miniature of the first. She named each one and made up relationships and stories about them in various combinations.

"So in another way, the doll was not simple at all. It was only simple in external appearance. Inside, it was almost infinite. She was not in a hurry to get to the core. She was busy weaving relationships and little adventures for her family of dolls. Eventually, though, she came to the very center. This doll was tiny and, for the first time, did not look like the other ones. This was a miniature, perfectly detailed baby.

"One day, a visitor, a traveler seeking shelter, stopped at the cottage and saw the little girl's family of dolls. He had seen many such nesting toys, but never had he seen the tiny baby. He knew it to be special, a talisman that would grant special favor in the life of its owner. He offered the family money for the doll, but they would not part with their daughter's favorite toy and were puzzled at the offer. Many days later, an old woman that the family knew to be a healer who lived deeper in the woods where she could find her herbs came to visit. She held the baby doll in her hand and said to the child, 'There will be people who will want this baby—to use it. Some would have it for selfish reasons, others for the good of many. It will be for you to decide who deserves the influence the baby carries . . . for it can be an influence to good or an influence to evil.' Indeed, the little girl remembered the visitor and had also had a presentiment that she would someday have a responsibility to pass the doll on, but to whom or why she had not known.

"It was not until she was sixteen that she had to choose. She was at her birthday party, and the old woman, now ancient, appeared at her side and said, 'You are a woman now and in no need of a little girl's toys. The time has come. Choose wisely.' And into the room came two princesses, each claiming rights to the toy, especially the baby. The princesses were twins, looking exactly alike, but the girl knew one to be good, the other evil. But how could she know which was which? She must decide, and she must decide correctly, for she was allied with the side of virtue in this world. It was a heavy responsibility.

"Suddenly, my mother snatched the book from my hands and snapped it shut. She was very angry with me. I saw something dangerous in her eyes before she turned and walked away with the book."

"Oh . . . so you never found out what the girl decided?"

"No wonder I'm so screwy, eh? Wrecked my life." She laughed, but there was an edge to her laugh.

"So," she continued, "if you apply all that lit crit to my story, and believe me I have . . . in spades . . . the analysis is very like that for your story."

"Yes, I can see that it might be . . . though the ambiguous ending . . ."

"No, that doesn't really matter. It's back to the choice and the protection and the passing down of the idea, or theme, as you put it. Same, really."

Once again, we just looked at each other for a long time. Then I ventured, "So the book can be positive or somehow corrupting. The sense of violation and possessiveness your mother felt, the sense of loss I felt . . . after reading addictively for days . . . I felt like what's his name in Tolkien . . . Gollum, when he lost the ring." She was nodding slowly, watching me put it together. "And the geeks who came to your house want it, for . . . I'm guessing, some kind of social manipulation, like the baby talisman, in some way I don't yet understand. While you . . . you're interested in the positive—the magic—which in literary terms has to do with the mystery of the creative process, thus the metaphor of the muse. That's what you're interested in protecting, to get back to your dissertation, preserving the heritage of creativity and the rich rewards of stories and all their subtle and elusive influences. Am I in the ballpark?"

"Home run, Charles. Home run."

We sat there at the table, thinking while looking at nothing in particular. After a while I asked her, "You never owned the book, did you?"

"No, my parents were protecting me from those corrupting influences."

"But you read it anyway."

"The first time I got my hands on it I was nine. Imagine how crafty I had become by twelve. By then, unbeknownst to them, I had read probably one hundred stories from that book."

"Do you feel it is yours now?"

"I don't know the answer to that, Charles. My parents were right about how it makes a person obsessive. And I have been, Lord knows. So I'm not sure what's the best . . . the safest thing to do."

"Are you in danger now . . . from those geek thugs?"

She looked frankly into my eyes and answered very quietly, "I think so, yes. They certainly assume the book to be in my possession. I'm sorry to have dragged you into it, my father and I. When it comes down to it, we are not so well suited to cloak and dagger stuff."

"Were you comfortable on the couch earlier?"

She smiled. "Yes, quite. I felt very safe and cozy."

"Guess I better get some sheets and blankets." I got up and walked toward the linen closet.

"Thank you, Charles."

I turned and shrugged. What was there really to say at this point?

She pointed to her backpack on the floor in the living room and said, "Well, at least I brought my own toothbrush."

"Good thing. I'm not so good with sharing mine."

We smiled in easy truce, and I added, "Do I need to show you around the rest of the house?"

She lifted one shoulder and said, "I've pretty much been through all the rooms. Never guessed the book would be hidden in such plain sight. But you'll be happy to know it's there in my backpack with my toothbrush. Do you want me to put it back where I found it?"

"Not yet, Celeste. Let's leave it there for the time being . . . but . . . thank you."

We were standing almost two rooms from each other during this exchange.

"Sheets," I said, turning back to the closet.

"And sleep."

"Yes, I'm ready."

"Me too."

SIX

It was not a restful night. Between doubts, convoluted analyses, things I should have said, the awareness that Celeste was sleeping in the other room—sleeping, I hoped, and not stealing everything I owned—incredulity, and a general unease about the whole set of circumstances, sleep was hard to come by. I am not a stranger to insomnia, but getting up and watching an old film with herbal tea wasn't an option. Eventually, I did sleep but with weird paranoid dreams of house cats turned into large predatory beasts . . . in my house.

I got up, just after six, feeling sluggish. I walked quietly through the house and heard tapping from my office. Looking in the door, I felt a flash of emotion—some lightning combination of fear and anger and betrayal. Celeste was typing at my computer station on my old-fashioned keyboard.

She must have heard my intake of breath because she turned and smiled and said, "Good morning. I tried not to wake you."

"Uh, you didn't . . . what . . ."

"Oh," she said with sudden understanding. "I couldn't sleep, and since I happen to be aware that I made your computer crash with my security, I thought I should fix it. Look, there's no damage; I just have a script there that overloads an intruder's search and makes their computer shut off for a while, and, well, there's a little wrinkle I added to punish them for snooping. So anyway, all's well. You're back in business."

I was still thickheaded and said, "But how did you get on? It's password protected."

She laughed. "You're such an English major. Luckily I minored in information technology." Then she added more seriously, "Don't trust me yet, do you?"

"I desperately need coffee."

It was true. Just the smell of dark-roast beans grinding would stimulate my various catatonic body systems, though the shock of seeing her in my office had jump-started the process. I went straight to the kitchen with the picture of Celeste stuck in my head, gracefully half-turned in the light of the computer screen in some old, thin warm-up pants and top she must have slept in. How well had she packed anyway?

I made the coffee strong and in plenty. If she didn't want any, I would be happy to have an extra couple of cups. I had a feeling my brain was going to need all the caffeine supercharging I could give it.

I thought she would join me, but when she didn't, I took her a cup, guessing she would want it the way I like it, strong but slightly sweet with real cream. It wasn't ego; I was just tired enough to suspend disbelief and reckoned that "this story" as she called it would have that congruity.

She was still in front of the computer, elbow on desk, chin in hand, staring intently.

"Uh oh," she muttered.

"I don't like the sound of that."

She turned again toward me (yes, gracefully) and said, "Well, I'm not sure. Is that coffee for me?"

I handed her the coffee, and she took a tentative sip and then looked up at me, saying, "The kind of coffee a person likes says a lot about them. There's a whole pseudopsychology about it, quite insightful really."

I could tell now that she was joking in that understated way of hers.

"Do you like it?"

She took another sip and seemed to withhold her judgment as if to tease me before saying simply, "Yes, I do."

I pulled another chair over next to hers and under the auspices of the Alliance of the Coffee Bean asked, "So what's the concern?"

"The geek thugs, as you've christened them, are trying to track me down."

"Can they find you here?"

"Not yet. I'm on your computer as you. But before long, they'll get curious about your attempt to access my system."

"What's with them, anyway? Why do they want the book? How do they even know about it?"

She pushed back from the desk and spun the chair to face me. She looked at me and shook her head. "My fault," she sighed. "Again, my fault."

I waited expectantly.

"I told you I was an IT minor. Well, I had this really brilliant boyfriend—an IT major. He has since become one of the most influential minds in IT development and is co-owner of one of the most powerful companies that controls computers, internet, VR, all of it. At first, though, he seemed so bright and charming and interested in what I cared about. I thought he would be a partner in this. Imagine an ally in the high-tech industry that understood what our culture was losing while it hurtled forward. Imagine such a person who was committed to marrying the old ethos with the new. He wasn't what he seemed . . ."

I sipped my coffee to allow her time to continue, but she had fallen silent, looking down into her cup, as if trying to decipher meaning hidden there.

I whispered, "The evil princess."

Celeste looked up at me and gave an almost imperceptible nod.

We sat for several more minutes in silence. Then I took her cup and went and refilled both and returned.

She said, "He is a bad man . . . a villain in the story."

"How could you have loved him, then?"

"Because the worst villains are most like us. Our own flaws mask theirs. His ambition was like mine, really. And I don't think he started with me falsely. We were close. Very. I brought him into the world of the book, but the book's potential began gnawing at him . . . bent him."

"It almost seems like the book is more dangerous than good," I put in.

"No, you mustn't think that. Remember your own analysis of the loss of cultural literacy. The book can be a powerfully rich, evocative, sweet reminder to the world of the contributions of the literary muse. Her magic."

"But what can the geeks do with it?"

"Remember, it reflects the reader. So if the reader is an acolyte of technology, a true believer that instant, short, efficient, pragmatic communication is the way we need to go, the book will mirror that. Worse, it will model that, showing them futures where the change is complete. In that way, the book will imagine its own demise. And these fools, who believe in the manifest destiny of the new and the worthlessness of the past, want to see that happen. They want to make it happen. They will be players in bringing about the new order and thus will be powerful. That's Ray's motivation now."

"Ray's your ex-boyfriend."

"Deathray, I call him."

"Deathray, eh? Okay, what do we do? How do we outsmart these guys?"

"We?"

"Well, since I couldn't bring myself to poison you—and these guys will come knocking on my door sometime soon—it may as well be we. I just don't know where to start. They seem relentless somehow, judging from how they treated your dad."

"Was it bad? Oh, I feel so guilty!"

"No, no, they just grabbed his arm. They didn't rough him up like in the movies."

"Not that that's beyond them, believe me."

"So . . . do we have some advantage? Something they don't have?"

"The book."

"Of course, the book, but that's what they're after. That's why they're coming. That's a disadvantage, if you ask me."

"No. Listen, we have the book, not as an object but as a tool."

"And . . . so we do what with it?"

"We read it."

"I'm not following."

"If it will help them get what they want by modeling it, it should do the same for us. That's the advantage."

"We'll have a coach! But which one of us should read it?"

"We read it together . . . aloud."

-

After a light breakfast, we went over to the couch and, like synchronized robots, sat down next to each other. Our elbows and upper arms were pressed together. It felt like an intense electric current was buzzing between the connection. Not in the least unpleasant. We looked at each other with surprise, but neither of us pulled away. Then Celeste reached up with her other hand and slowly, firmly pushed me away.

She put on an English accent and said, "My word, Professor, if it's to be a matter of mere mutual attraction, we may as well give up the book now and forget all about doing the right thing to save civilization."

"Quite right," I replied, going along. "Mustn't start mucking about and getting distracted. Straight on, stiff upper lip and all that. Tally ho."

I edged away a bit as she reached into her backpack and retrieved the book. I caught my breath when I saw it. I wanted to take it out of her hands, but folded mine tightly in my lap and watched as she placed it on hers. We both looked curiously at the cover. Nothing. Nor on the spine.

"Curiouser and curiouser," she quoted.

She slowly opened the cover, and the pages appeared blank. Then they seemed to start moving . . . that is not physically moving, but the surface seemed to flow. Her words caused me to associate it with the Cheshire Cat coming out of transparency—only this was like a hundred images cycling rapidly into semivisibility, now paragraphs, now pictures, now a blur. She snapped the book closed.

"We need to focus, I think. Maybe it can't read us—I mean there're two readers now . . . and . . . well, maybe that little spark we just felt is causing an ambivalence of purpose or something—"

Just then there was a sharp knock on my front door. I looked at Celeste, and she suddenly wore a mask of genuine fear. She bolted for the back rooms while I went slowly toward the door, feeling strangely anxious.

I opened the door about a foot and saw two youngish men standing there, the two I had seen accosting Mr. Lathke. One of them was certainly Ray.

"Yes?"

"Hello, sir. We're looking for Celeste Lathke and thought you might know where we might find her."

"Why would you think such a thing?"

"I'm afraid we can't talk about that. Is she here?"

"No, she isn't."

"We heard voices."

"Have you ever heard of virtual-reality equipment?"

"We practically invented it."

"Well then, you know that one can speak to other people with it."

"We happen to know that you know her."

"You know no such thing."

"You tried to hack into her computer system."

"Surely you know enough logic to see that that does not make her an acquaintance. She has written academic work in my field—work I find intellectually suspect, mixing literary criticism with sociology. A dubious combination I'm sure you would agree. I was trying to find out more about her work and qualifications. How is it that you know I went looking? Are you the computer police? Have you ever heard of the literary character Big Brother?"

"We build, run, and maintain the system. We need to watch activity that may threaten it."

"You're like God, then."

"God is dead."

"No one reads Nietzsche anymore."

"We'd like to come in," he said and pushed on the door.

My foot was behind it, and it sprang back and hit him in the forehead. He glared at me with a malevolence that he seemed to have difficulty controlling.

"You'll regret that, Professor."

"I don't know you. I don't know Celeste Lathke. You're obviously following a blind alley in your search."

I shut the door firmly but realized my hands were shaking. I turned the deadbolt and walked into the rear of the house. I found Celeste, not cowering but frantically turning off and disconnecting my computer network.

"What are you doing?"

"He's not done with you."

"What do you mean? Surely he could see they're on the wrong trail."

She kept working, saying, "A. They're not on the wrong trail, even if they don't know it yet. B. Ray is a vindictive SOB, and he will try to punish you just for standing up to him. He's gonna surge your system, and it will be very soon."

"Surge my system?"

"From his mobile unit he has the capability of doing all kinds of mischief and damage, including directing a power surge through your network and frying the whole thing. Hang on . . ."

I watched her double-check her work and then pick up my mobile that was sitting on the desk and switch it off.

"We'll have to go dark for a while . . . which actually works in our favor. He'll think he's paid you back and then will forget about you for a while. It should give us some time."

"To do what? You saw what the book did."

"We were conflicted then. I think Ray has just provided us some focus. Come on."

We went back to the couch, me by way of the window where I saw the geeks' car turning a corner down the block. I joined her where she was standing by the couch.

"Intellectually suspect?"

"Improvising . . . I . . ." She laughed, which broke some of the tension.

We sat again in unison, careful not to touch, and she once again opened the book. It flashed again, but quickly resolved into a title page. Celeste began reading.

The Blade of Sacrifice
By Ari del Canto

One priest held the quivering animal while the other held the knife in the air for all to see. Down it flashed, efficiently, mercifully killing the beast. Up again flew the blade, now red, and all knew the god was placated. And they also knew that if the priests carried out the remainder of the ceremony with equal dispatch and reverence, the god would bless them all. The blood was poured off into a stone channel, and the heart deftly removed and placed on the highest carved stone that reached up into the open sky. And, yes, down from on high, like the knife, came the eagle to pluck up the bloody sacrificial heart and transport it into the sky dwelling of the god. All was well; the interlocking spheres of earth, sea, and air were reinforced once more. Reverently, the people lifted their eyes and voices, chanting the ancient paean of praise of the god. And then they went to their homes.

The priests turned from the altar, too, while acolytes cleaned it and prepared the remains of the sacrificed animal. The priests would feast this evening. Why should they not? Though they could see the eagle high in a tree at the edge of the forest blasphemously shredding the sacrificial heart, were not the people content? Were not the priests responsible for this contentment, even the very stability of the civilization? Of what importance was it then that the paean was not ancient, nor the rituals of the sacrifice itself? The people had short memories and were content, happy that the priests had given them equanimity. Into their opulent chambers went the priests to eat and drink with their concubines, seemingly content as well with their power.

In the evening, when the fires had grown dim and the priests and their concubines had grown equally dull and sated, firelight was reflected along the blade of a raised knife, the same ceremonial knife. Down it came once more. Up it rose again, red. Then, there was but one contented priest, the sole priest of the land. It was what he had wanted all along. His dead brother priest, his brother in life, did not know of this desire, for he had been complacent in his shared power, exalted above the people and able with his brother to direct the country where they would.

Were the priests evil? Were they but willing mediators between the people and their beliefs? There was one priest remaining, and of the two, he could indeed be said to be the closer to evil.

In his reign, this High Priest, as he styled himself, saw that the god required more sacrifice, and so where before there was one sacrifice per moon, then there became two. The variety of sacrificial animals increased. And the feasts after were more splendid. In time, the demands of the god, according to his High Priest, became ever greater. But the people remained quiescent, for the god had visited no calamities on them.

There was a man whose job it was to procure for the temple the sacrificial animals. He was neither priest nor farmer, rather a sort of agent between. Thus, he could see the states of both temple and farm, priest and people. He understood the High Priest to be drifting into deeper and deeper evil, for which the country must eventually pay. This man, though, had no power to oppose the priest; he had no power at all, whereas the priest was all powerful. There were no other power structures within the country that might do so, nor were the people of a politically sophisticated nature in governance or revolution. Only the agent saw the evil, the corruption, and the growing greed that was sapping the strength of his country. All he could do was provide sacrificial animals. He saw that the capacity of the people to provide sacrifices for the temple must eventually be outstripped, and someday they would be impoverished. It would be many years, however. Poverty and hunger were only very slowly spreading like an invasive plant, unnoticeable.

The agent could do but one thing to hasten change. He could provide more and more animals. He could stimulate the High Priest's appetite for excess. He could give him all he wanted and more and thus hasten his demise by emptying the well of animals. He must hope that the resilience of the people would save them, that their old beliefs would have resurgence were they not too long forgotten. The way to defeat the High Priest's evil would be to feed it, for evil is never really satisfied; it is ever more voracious.

The High Priest and his many concubines grew fatter and fatter, the sacrifices more and more frequent, the feasts more debauched as the agent provided more and more animals, until at last there was only a single scrawny beast to sacrifice. It was a pathetic creature, full of sores and blemishes. It enraged the High Priest when he saw it there on the altar. He screamed futilely and waved his blade at his acolytes until his own swollen heart burst under the strain of his rage. Down he fell at the foot of the altar above the dismayed populace, dead and unseeing the blue heavens above his open eyes. Down, too, flew the eagle, landing and plucking out those selfsame eyes, eating them in horrible gore and spectacle before flying off with a shriek.

The agent forced himself to mount the steps and turn to face the people, for he was a humble man. He spoke quietly so the people had to lean in tightly to hear. He spoke of the green earth and their crops of grain and fruit and vegetables, reminding them that they were yet fruitful and could turn from the slaughter of animals and remember their earlier gods of gentleness and wisdom that their grandparents had honored.

The agent finished speaking, hoping the people would recover. He left the place of the temple, for he no longer had a livelihood and must find a new one. But he was content.

Celeste closed the book, looked up, and said, "Never read anything like that in here before. Must be your weird influence."

"Mine? Hey, I'm a romantic. You're the one who started this cosmic dispute with the geek thugs."

"Shut up, you tweed-wearing, pipe-smoking, lit-spouting academic."

"Oh, let's not get personal, you breaking-and-entering, computer-hacking bibliothief."

"Bibliothief? Couldn't you just call me a book thief?"

"Word bandit."

"Library footpad."

"Manuscript pickpocket."

"Tome robber."

"Tome robber . . . that's good! Okay you win, now what?"

"Well, since it's been established that you are a tweed-wearing—"

"I do not wear tweed, madam, and I do not smoke."

"One for three, then. But you are a lit-spouting academic; ergo I suggest you do what you do."

"To wit?"

"Analyze this charming, if not romantic, story of ours. What's it mean, and more importantly, what does it imply we are to do?"

"Ah, I see. Allow me a moment to ruminate on the conundrum."

"Ruminate away. Light a pipe if it would help."

I glared at her and then ventured, "Okay, thematically, we have these two evil guys who become more evil as they gain more power. One is a worse fellow, greedier, willing to do violence even unto his brother, Cain-like, perhaps a sociopath in modern terms. He is unstoppable in conventional ways, and he, for wholly egotistical reasons, hijacks the unsuspecting, even complicit culture."

"Surely he also at least half-believes he is worthy of his position vis-à-vis the gods and people?"

"Yes, certainly he does, as do all dictators and cult leaders. So, to continue, he is only vulnerable by getting what he wants . . . or too much of what he wants. Since he deserves it all, he has no limits on what he will take, to his own detriment. Right so far?"

"Elementary, my dear Watson. Press on."

"Patience. Now let us turn to our current predicament. We, too, are faced with two ambitiously unbalanced, powerful fellows who seek to remold the world in their image and hold it firmly under their control. I would venture to say that your soulmate, Ray, or Deathray as you futuristically monikered him, is the more driven of the two. I am correct, am I not, that it was he and not his mute partner that harangued me a while ago?"

"Yes, that was his voice, for sure."

"So, following our story, Ray being the more dangerous must be helped to take full control. Counterintuitive, I know, but this then hastens the evil he would perpetrate, while his megalomania would make him underestimate and discount opposition, giving rise to over-reaching on his part. And then he must be fed . . . until he pops."

Celeste sat still for a moment, contemplating my brilliant analysis, and then she said, "You still haven't answered my question."

"Which was?"

"What are we to do?"

"Oh, that. Hey, I shouldn't have to do all the heavy lifting. Feel free to pitch in anytime."

"All right, how about this . . . Ray and his buddy, whose real name I don't know but everyone always has called Maurice, want this non-literate society, wholly cut off from the complex lessons to be read in history and the insights of literature—thus psychology and philosophy. In short, they want people to live in the hedonistic moment, who are thereby completely dependent on the superstructure of the society—"

"Controlled by these guys."

"Exactly, and it is a population that cannot imagine a different existence because they have never been able to study anything with their stunted attention span and illiteracy."

"It seems to me," I replied, "judging from our current state of affairs, we are more than halfway there already. It's an old theme after all. So what do Ray and Maurice need of this one book?"

She smiled conspiratorially. "Here's the rub for them. They, too, are infected with their own philosophy and therefore lack sufficient imagination to fully envision this brave new world of theirs. Sure, they have the technical savvy, but not the long-term, big picture 'story' of that emerging culture. Thus, they need the power of the book to give them that image."

"And then destroy the book?"

"Oh, no, I doubt that. They will see it as the precious, secret talisman. It will be their private, inscrutable god. They will probably even fear it, but they won't dare harm it. With atrophied imaginations, they might need it again someday. But only that one book."

"So, as has already begun to happen, the rest of the books, and what they teach, disintegrate through disuse by way of the simple expedients of technical immediacy and intimacy—and laziness—the pictures and vocalizations, the faux reality, with which the population entertains itself. So our friends, Ray and Maurice, become in effect the barbarians who burn the libraries."

"Yes, though we can't give them all the credit—or even much of the credit, for that matter. They're just harvesting a crop that was planted long ago. A difference from the barbarian hordes is that the libraries still exist in the digital domain; they are just not used."

"But even thwarting the geek thugs does little to stop the snowball that's rolling down the hill."

"I've missed talking to someone who peppers his speech with metaphors."

"She says metaphorically."

We were smiling at our shared pleasure of dialogic analysis, but then a shadow crossed her brow.

"What?" I asked, concerned.

"We still haven't answered the question."

Together we declaimed, "What are we to do?"

We laughed and then went silent.

Then I said, "You know, we have to make a series of decisions."

"Hmm?"

"We need, first, to decide if we're up to continuing this battle . . . 'cause that's what it's shaping up to be. If so, we need to decide if we're really going to use the knife story as a model. And if we do, we need to somehow figure a way to isolate Ray and, of course, come up with what we will give him to make him succeed and ultimately fail. We have to, in Hamlet's words, 'delve one yard below their mines and blow them at the moon.'"

"That quotation is the point of saying yes to the battle. The society that Ray is trying to bring about, which as you say is already upon us, would not, will not, have ready access to Hamlet's machinations. That's why we need to oppose these guys. It's not that we're Luddites. I love technology and VR and all that stuff; it can be such a useful tool—but not as a replacement for all the literature and history you were talking about, the mental exercise of imagination that happens through immersive reading. As for using the story, that, too, seems a given. If we are fighting to save literature, we use literature. If the book is what they need, it is our best weapon."

"Okay, we're agreed." I reached out to shake hands with formal affectation and went on, "Now, as to isolating Ray. I think we do that by treating initially with Maurice exclusively."

"Oh, that'll piss off Ray."

"Enough, I hope, that he elbows Maurice to the side. Our first step in feeding his megalomania."

"Ooh, very wicked, Charles. Where did you learn to be so devious?"

"Shakespeare, Poe, Machiavelli . . . the usual suspects."

"Not so usual these days . . . which again is our point. But wait," she added, glancing at the ceiling in concentration, "their advantage is that they have absolutely free access and control over computers and communications. They can virtually see our every move, listen to every communication, subvert our every endeavor. We need a way to neutralize that advantage—hang on . . . Oh! So just like going dark like we are now, we should get away from all these electronic nodes, virtual-reality corridors, and links to triangulating satellites."

"I agree with the idea, but what do you mean?"

"Road trip to the country, Charles. We choose our ground like any number of great generals you can read about in the history books. And our ground, the place the geeks will feel least comfortable, is outside the city."

"Big camper are you?"

"We actually did go camping a lot. You remember how old-fashioned my father is. Nothing like a camping trip in the woods with a carload of books."

I said, "Believe it or not, I actually grew up in . . . well, near the country and camped too. But what about communication and stuff?"

"Oh, we take our gadgets along, but they will only be of limited value to us, and more importantly, to them, in the country."

"So . . . ?"

"We pack, decide where to go, and . . . go."

"Wait, but won't that favor them? I mean, they'll have us away from help, witnesses, out in the middle of nowhere."

"What, these guys are gonna track us and disembowel us with their scout knives? They only know how to do that virtually. They're gamers, and games—even VR games—are a lot different from being out in the woods with snakes and bears and having to deal with food and tents and mosquitoes and . . ."

"Defecation."

"Ticks."

"Sunburn."

"Poison oak."

"Fording rivers."

"Climbing sheer cliffs."

"Felling trees."

"Felling trees? Where does that come into it?"

"Oh . . . yeah, probably no felling of trees. It just seemed so outdoorsy . . . manly."

"Non-geeky?"

"Exactly. Geeks don't know squat about felling trees."

"Do you?"

"As a wee lad, I imbibed the story of Paul Bunyan and Babe the Blue Ox."

"Oh, I see. So you know your way around tree chopping, for sure."

"You betcha, eh?"

"So where should we go?"

"I have no idea."

SEVEN

"It's not just the man behind the curtain, is it?"

She looked over at me, brushing her windblown hair off her face. "What?"

"Oz. We've been talking about Ray—the evil wizard behind the curtain. It's true that you always need to mistrust the man behind the curtain, his motives, ambitions, and all. The rise of dictators. But this Oz of his, too, this one-world government of the digitized world is what's really scary."

"What, he's—or it's—the Antichrist now?"

"Hmm. Well, okay, maybe I'm going off the deep end a little. And here I'd been thinking of you as the zealot."

"Oh ho! Me a zealot? You're telling me this now while we're racing north in this dilapidated vehicle? You're silent for the last hundred miles and then start talking about the Wizard of Oz and the Antichrist, and I'm a zealot. You know, Professor, you are an ass."

"Geez. Down girl. I was . . . uh . . . philosophizing. And anyway, remember how we got into this mess. In point of fact, you are a bloody zealot . . . cloak and dagger, breaking and entering, guys chasing you."

"Those are real guys, Sherlock . . . and they're after you too."

"Thank you very much for that, by the way."

"I knew it."

"What's that supposed to mean? You mean, like, men are all alike or some such?"

"They are enough to make it an aphorism."

"You call that an aphorism? I thought you were college educated."

"How 'bout this then? Ad hominem does not well suit one of your august profession."

"How about I just drive—oh, wait, you're a woman; you probably have to pee. Should I pull over?"

"Are you really going to compete for the last word in this ridiculous little spat?"

"I'll stop if you stop."

"I'll show you mine if you show me yours."

We held each other's eyes for a long second and then both started laughing hysterically.

After chuckling for a couple of miles, I said, "Okay then, we've established that our mutual point of reference is the playground. Good."

"Oh, yeah, we're bound to prevail in this quest against the geek thugs."

"I had the sense of arrested development from those guys, so maybe we're on to something. Reduce it all to a game of dodgeball."

"I think your earlier suggestion was the best."

"What was that?"

"Just drive."

So I did for many more miles, until I saw the little green sign and said, "Okay, I give. I'm pulling into this rest stop. My bladder is gonna explode."

Celeste smiled in restrained triumph.

I poked her in the side. "You have to go too, don't you?"

"Desperately."

-

We were sprawled on the shady grass of the kind of gorgeous rest stop found in the Pacific Northwest. We were well into Oregon now, having driven for about six hours from the outskirts of San Francisco, where this whole escapade had begun. (It's late, I know, to give this geographical information, but until now, it has not mattered. In literature, spirit of place only matters when it matters. It has begun to matter.)

We had gathered my old camping gear, such food and clothes as she had with her in her backpack, and what we could rustle from my closets and pantry, then packed my old hybrid Toyota. And then sat and waited . . . and, irresolute . . . waited into the night . . . and then slept. We left the city at four in the morning, still without a plan except to head somewhere north. When you're on the west coast of the continent, options narrow. West was a giant ocean, south was obviously out being increasingly urban, east turns into desert before long, so north looked the obvious choice. Besides, we had both spent time in the Pacific Northwest, and we figured that Ray would be least comfortable in all that open country and forest. So here we were dozing in a rest stop between Klamath Falls and Crater Lake. It was still only ten a.m.

After a while, Celeste said, "I guess now that we're away, we're not in a hurry. I mean we have the book, they don't know where we are, we don't have a plan yet, so we probably should take our time and really drop off the map for a bit."

I rolled onto my side and looked at her. "So just vacation for a while? Seems odd inasmuch as we have decided we're in some kind of grand war."

"Wars fought hastily are wars lost."

"Lao Tzu?"

"Me."

"Hmm, deep. Okay, well, since we decided to go inland and get off the main artery of Highway 5, I do remember up here a ways above Bend and in the Cascades there's a little lake my family camped at once."

"How far? I'm already sick of the car."

"It's a bit of a fer piece, maybe another several hours or more, but we could get there this afternoon."

"A fer piece? Are you channeling Davy Crockett now?"

"Shut up and go to the bathroom again, then let's go."

"Yep, I guess we better use these highfalutin facilities before we start bushwhacking. What's the name of the place we're going, anyway, Davy?"

"Clear Lake, little missy, Clear Lake."

-

With a mere look, Celeste nixed my idea of a side trip to Crater Lake, so we continued north, stopping once for gas and paying with cash so as to leave no electronic trail. We drove up that wide valley between the peaks and hidden lakes, turning the corner at Lava Butte and up toward Bend, the scent of pine heavy in the air. Then we headed up into the foothills to the beautiful historic forest and ranchlands of Sisters with the view of its namesake Three Sisters peaks, and then on northwest, deeper and deeper into the conifer-covered mountains.

If we forgot for a time our weighty mission, it was due to the serenity of the landscape that poured in through our open windows, the narrowing roads decreasing our speed and commensurately intensifying the grandeur of the scenery. I had put on Mozart's *Requiem* as we passed through Sisters, and the swelling double fugue blended with the beautiful sights and rarefied scent of pine forest. We received occasional vistas of the still snow covered peak, Mount Jefferson, lakes, and buttes.

And in that long drive, few words were spoken more than Celeste's quiet comment, "This is why they invented national parks."

In time, we came to the junction of Highway 126, the McKenzie, and turned due south, and the dormant memories of childhood awoke in my mind. Before I could see it, I could feel Clear Lake on my left. I knew just when to look to see it emerge from the trees. I knew right where the turn at the south end of the lake would be, crossing the stream and easing slowly into the nearly deserted campground on the eastern shore. Although I couldn't be certain, I think I found the very campsite of old at the edge of the woods quite close to the lake. It was three in the afternoon.

Like a couple of old hands, we set up my family's big four-man tent, threadbare with age but waterproof. My parents and older brother seemed almost to be nearby, gathering firewood or setting up the camp stove. Celeste, too, moved in a dream of nostalgia, occasionally smiling at some private thought. When we were done, we went down to the water's rim and sat on a log to watch the sun dip down toward the trees, which were reflected perfectly in the lake mirror.

We still had spoken very little, and I began to suspect that it was because speaking would bring us round to our situation, our problems, our uncertainties. Better to be quiet and pretend we were here for the rejuvenating properties of nature. Perhaps we were. I was prepared to believe it. Celeste almost seemed hypnotized by the view and barely registered it when I got up and went back to camp. I returned with more of the riesling in plastic camping cups, which we shared while the shadows of the trees on the opposite bank reached out toward us, closer and closer.

When they were at our feet, I said, "We had a canoe when we camped here. We went out at just this time, and the lake was glassy like this, so still and quiet. We spoke in whispers and tried not to knock our paddles against the boat. Then we saw this huge osprey soaring over the lake, not high, really. Suddenly, it dove down quite near us . . .

splash! It came up with a fish in its talons and flew over to a tree to eat. I still remember the look on the faces of my family, watching that bird come down in the orange light."

Celeste nodded and said, "Yes, I've been thinking of our little family, too . . . out in woods like this. My father knew all about the birds." Her voice caught at the end of this sentence; her eyes welled. "My father . . . I shouldn't have left him. I should just give Ray and Maurice the damn book. What if they hurt him?"

I had no answer, of course, so I put my arm around her shoulders, and she leaned into me. The sun set in stillness.

We made a light dinner under lantern light and then somewhat awkwardly prepared for bed—rather tatty sleeping bags atop unstable air mattresses.

"I'm glad you brought your own toothbrush."

"Yes, me too. I seem to recall that you are not so good with sharing yours."

"No, you have to know someone at least a week before you start the cavalier sharing of toothbrushes."

"Very sensible. You never know where that toothbrush has been."

"Indeed."

"Charles?"

"Yes?"

"Would you read me a story?"

"Do you think it's wise?"

"Who knows."

"Okay, let's see if the book will be nice to us tonight. Get it out."

She dug into her backpack, pulled the book out, and handed it to me with an enigmatic expression on her face. I think it was a symbolic act . . . returning it, in a way, into my keeping. We reclined on our respective beds.

There was an engraved ship on the cover of the thin volume. I opened to the title page and read: *The Little Rajão.*

Then I turned to the first page, saw that the text was illustrated with the most delicate colored drawings, and began.

23 August 1879, in the Pacific, aboard the Ravenscrag

Oh, what a magical morning this is! The dawn is coming up on this tropic sea, and Papa has guaranteed that this would be the day of our sighting of the islands of the little Kingdom of Hawaii! I don't know how I can contain myself . . . all these weeks at sea and what we've seen and passed through. It is almost too much. I'm afraid Momma was rather cross with me when I woke so early. But, really, how can she not be thrilled by the poetry of this grand day? And when I think back on the ice and storms of the Cape, oh, my stomach does a turn. All that contrasted with this indescribable blue. And to arrive on my birthday . . . perfect!

But we are going so slowly! There is no wind to assist the steam, and we seem to be practically drifting. Papa laughed just now at my impatience. The ogre. I shall punish him by going to the "tween-decks" steerage to visit my friends. I don't care if he and Momma don't approve of a "well-bred girl associating with rag-amuffin foreigner immigrants." Bah, just because Papa's cousin is the captain. We're not English aristocracy after all . . . just American cousins who happened to spend a year there putting on airs. I'm so glad P & M were both bilious while rounding the Horn, or I'd never have been set sufficiently free to meet my "Portagee" friends.

I am twelve this day and certainly grown enough to go where I please on this little boat! I had already missed so much of their good company between Madeira and Chile when I was able to sneak away to make their acquaintance. Momma accuses me of slumming, and it is true that the immigrants live in quite poor estate, but it isn't why I go there. My friend, Maria Dias, who is nine, cautioned me to use our first-class lavatory before coming down, as theirs up in the fo'c'sle makes the women seasick almost every time they enter it. I occasionally get a whiff about their clothes, and it is enough to put one off her feed. They have to share the same water cup with everyone in their compartment... twenty-three, I think. So Momma need not worry overmuch that I'll forget to come back to our stately cabin.

But she is wrong to think that they are low people when they are but poor. They are giving and full of fun, especially Maria's mother, whose name is Maria, too, so I shan't get the names crossed... and both her father and brother are named Jose ... I wouldn't want to be named Eliza like Momma! What I love best is when Mister Dias and his two friends play and sing. Each has a little guitar of a different size, like the three bears: momma guitar, papa guitar, and baby guitar. Ha! Only they aren't guitars but have names I can't pronounce because they are Portagee words. I was interested, and so Maria wrote their names on a scrap of paper. They are, *braguinha, rajão, viola de arame.* The last one is the most poetical name, but it is the biggest, so I like the momma best. It is the strumming one, while the little baby with the gargoyle name takes the melody.

When the weather is fine, we all sit atop the fo'c'sle head and have a merry time singing and doing the Madeira folk dance, though Momma complains that I am getting as brown as a nut from the sun. But sometimes the breeze blows the coal smoke and dust right across the deck and we are driven below... or then I make my privileged escape back to our promenade deck. And sometimes the weather is foul and there are clusters of women who are seasick for days, and the sailors are not sympathetic. Papa says I have a cast-iron stomach . . . which I think a good thing unless I should fall overboard and sink. Maria says that when it's rough, they try to stand up on the steps below the hatch, which is covered with canvas to keep the water from pouring in but does let in some fresh air, as below it is dreadful rank. But when we can, and it has been often, we enjoy the music, and I am beginning to learn some of their songs, though I don't know what the words I'm singing mean, nothing too terrible, I think. Maria says they are mostly about the countryside and island. Mister Nunes plays the momma instrument that I like, and he is a nice man. He sometimes lets me hold his *rajão* and shows me some chords. It is excellent fun!

Oh, what news! As I was writing, I had a note from the purser that my Portagee friends wished to say goodbye before we part company. So I dashed over to the fo'c'sle, though I know I'm not to run aboard ship, and they were there looking for the island on the horizon. Maria must have told them about my birthday, for they gathered around me and sang me a song. It was splendid and embarrassing at the same time. And then, while everyone clustered around me, Mister Diaz and Mister Nunes came forward and presented me with a gift. Oh, what a gift! It was the momma! My own beautiful rajão in a cunning little case. Oh, I shall treasure it always! I will become an expert!

Papa is calling me. Hawaii has been sighted!

I had been showing the illustrations to Celeste as we had finished each page, and now at the end, I turned once more toward her and found her eyes closed and a contented smile on her face.

"Do you want to see this last picture? I think the rajão is the precursor to the ukulele."

"Mmm . . . I can see it in my mind."

"Did you sleep through the end?"

"Um mm . . ."

I closed the book, tucked it into her backpack, and turned off the lantern. I felt nearly asleep too.

EIGHT

I woke to a pleasant confusion . . . unclear if I were child or adult. There was my family tent arched above me in faded green, the crisp, chill redolent of pine, the whirring sound of a camp stove. I turned to see who might be sleeping near me. Was it my brother, Larry? No, I was alone. I rolled over toward the door, which was flung wide to the tree-shaded campsite, sunbeams slanting in the higher branches and a still, golden lake beyond. Her back to me, there was a lithe woman, dressed as I had seen her another morning—was it two days ago? Celeste seemed to be making coffee in her feline way. I watched her, and it occurred to me that she blended into these woods better than in the city. I imagined she could spring off after a rabbit in a flash. I realized, too, becoming more and more the adult as I slowly woke, that she was a lovely creature. No, that was poetry. She was at that moment a lovely woman, attractive in all the ways a woman can be.

It was then that she sensed me watching and turned.

"He wakes. Rise, Paul Bunyan, and fell a tree for more firewood."

"Is that coffee?"

"Come find out."

"Bathroom, toothbrush."

"You and your dental hygiene. Chop, chop, it's almost ready."

"My dad used to say that."

On joining her, I received my steaming cup, prepared exactly as I like it, and nodded my appreciation of her memory. We went down to our log by the lake and watched the colors brighten as the day rose.

"Did you sleep well?"

"Mmm, I dreamed of my father's music shop when I was little."

"Probably the influence of that story last night."

"Probably. It was nice, though."

"Story or dream?"

"Both."

"Do you want to analyze the story?"

"Oh, not really. I'm sure we could tease out meaning about the cultural heritage being preserved and all that . . . the symbol of the little instrument. What was it?"

"Rajão, probably the precursor to the ukulele. Your father has some old instruments that are probably in that family."

"I would imagine he does. He seems to have one of everything."

"That's where this started for me, you know . . . your father's shop. I was getting my guitar adjusted."

"Oh, I guess I never asked. Sorry. You're a musician, then?"

"The word your father used was *dilettante*."

"Ha, he would use that word, wouldn't he? Genteel ambiguity."

"What about you?"

"What about me?"

"Do you play music?"

"Ah, music. It seems like a past life."

I waited for her to elaborate.

"I learned how to play quite a few of those instruments in the shop . . . not expertly, but well enough . . ."

"A *dilettante*?"

"Touché. Violin, though, was my main instrument. It was also the source of my first conflict with my father. He wanted me playing Vivaldi, and I wanted to play Irish fiddle tunes."

"O'Carolan?"

"You know him? His melodies are so beautiful!"

"I love Irish melodies and have played quite a bit of O'Carolan."

"Interesting."

"Isn't it? Finally, something we have in common. If this book thing doesn't work out, we can start a band."

We held each other's eyes for a moment, smiling, and clinked our coffee cups in a mock toast.

After a few minutes, I said, "You know, the semester is not quite over, and I'm gonna need to wrap up my classes. There's not much to do, really, but I have to make a bit of a virtual appearance."

"What, you mean teachers are still needed for some part of the education process? I thought students these days worked in peer groups and participated in discussions without the old teacher-centered interference."

"The blind leading the blind theory of higher ed. Yeah, that works so well. I can't tell you how satisfying it is to sit on my hands while the students reinforce each other's ill-conceived opinions. Why I bothered to get a PhD if I can't occasionally share my knowledge . . . as if lectures can't be really interesting. Hey, stop pushing my buttons!"

She smiled mischievously and said, "Okay, okay. Well, I suppose we'll have to get you some more direct satellite access pretty soon, but I'm pretty sure the Deathray will be scanning your activity for clues to my whereabouts. He casts a pretty wide net."

"We can wait a bit, I suppose. The students are just finishing up a project, so they won't begin to get panicky for a few days."

"Good. Let's get back to our vacation!"

"More coffee."

"Aye, laddie, more java."

"Joe."

"Bean brew."

"Mud."

"Hey now, no calling my coffee mud."

"Yes'm. So is there more?"

"Yep."

-

We were walking silently along the lake shore when we heard a strange clacking sound bouncing across the water. I recognized it and touched Celeste's shoulder while scanning the trees overhanging the water.

"There, two o'clock, low branch, belted kingfisher, male."

"What, you're Audubon now?"

"Shh . . . I told you we used to camp here. My dad was a birder too."

The jewel of a bird, his back brilliant sapphire in the sun, flew from the branch, hovered a faction of a second, and plunged headfirst into the water. Celeste gasped. Then the little bird, seeming so very out of his element, surfaced and flew back to the very branch he had left, this time with a small fish wiggling in his tightly clamped beak. He flipped the fish so it was tail out and, throwing his head back, gulped it down. It was efficient, businesslike even, and comical. The fish had been a third his size, and as he twitched and flicked his wet wings, it was easy to imagine that he was trying to adjust the fish in his tiny gullet.

"Halcyon," I said.

"Yeah, idyllic."

"Oh, yes, figuratively too."

"You're not referring to the pretty day . . . and maybe your memories of the good old days with your family?"

"Of course, but in that annoying academic way of mine—I say this so you won't have to—I am also referring to the origin of the word: a mythological bird, often associated with that bird, the kingfisher."

"You know what?"

"What?"

"You're right."

"About?"

"Annoying."

"I do like being right."

"Hmm, yes, I can see you do."

"But annoying?"

"Kinda."

"Shall we walk on?"

"Let's."

–

In that other sense, it was indeed a halcyon day, with perfectly still trees perched along the watery mirror, warm air, birds and squirrels hopping about in perfunctory pursuit of their duties, the rare reverberant call of a thrush deep in the woods, and we two, the only humans strolling companionably, chatting, remembering, and sitting in long woodland silences.

And the evening, too, held us in a piney bowl in which we spoke less and less. It was as if we were conspiring to ignore the reason we had come, as if it were some fiction once read and easily forgotten. So, too, were we conspiring to ignore the fact that there was, under the easy congeniality, that slow simmer of attraction, our commonalities gradually mingling like flavors in a sauté. Perhaps for that reason, we stayed by the fire late into the night, watching the embers glow and pulse like some magical city. It was refreshingly childlike as well, for adults rarely have the time to stare into a campfire. So we were nearly mesmerized and quite sleepy when we crawled into our sleeping bags in the dark tent. Only the dim orange glow of dying embers illumined Celeste's eyes as we said goodnight. It was the perfect time to kiss . . . but there was no kiss.

NINE

We woke to a cacophony of wind noises, nearby nylon flapping, pine needles whipping above, and lake water churning. We looked outside and then at each other. Neither of us needed to say what was on both our minds; the idyl was clearly over. We got to work before rain could make matters worse. Making coffee was not going to be a possibility, so we made a quick job of packing the car, jumped in, and drove out of the campground just as the first drops began to fall.

Thinking out loud, I said, "Well, we should get out of the mountains, I guess, but keep going north, yes?"

Celeste shrugged acquiescence.

"So . . . we'll take twenty back west, and I think it'll bend up north sort of parallel to the main highway."

"Uh hmm."

I looked over at her. "What?"

She gave me a thin smile and replied, "Oh, I guess I was feeling a little cheated. That was the first mental respite I've had in . . . well . . . it seems like forever. So . . . just too short." She forced herself to brighten and added, "But thank you, Charles, for the lovely camping trip."

Weaving through the rain-swept forest, I said, "Celeste . . ."

She touched my arm. "It's okay. It was just so nearly perfect."

Choosing not to explore that word, *nearly*, I said, "Halcyon."

"Oh, are we talking about birds again?"

"That's my girl."

"So, you know, it would probably have been drier had we gone back to the east side of the mountains."

"Okay, she's back. Might have been late snow back up higher crossing over."

"Snow . . . you realize it's nearly summer?"

"You wanna drive, then?"

"Oh, no, I prefer having a chauffeur . . . even if he doesn't know the territory."

"*The Music Man*?"

"Oh, very good, Charles. Full marks for you."

"So let's hear one of the songs and see how deep your knowledge of show tunes really is."

She immediately began singing in a thin but sweet soprano. She ended on a high, loud "Cheep!" and looked at me triumphantly.

"Bravo, Celeste, bravo! A woman of parts, I must say."

"Dilettante, you mean?"

"In the nicest possible way."

"Okay, then. Takes one to know one."

"Indeed."

Thus, we came winding out of the foothills into the farmland and the lessening of the rain. It was still quite blustery, but in a rather glorious way. We coasted into the quiet rural town of Sweet Home.

Seeing the name, Celeste murmured, "Don't I wish."

I spotted a hip-looking coffee place and announced, "We have officially arrived in the Pacific Northwest," and pulled in.

The place was partially filled with people sipping coffee, and there was a low murmur of voices. Nearly everyone was wearing a VR headset and engaged in some kind of isolated conversation or playing a game. The contrast with the kind of conversation Celeste and I had had by the lake was jarring.

Ensconced with scones and French roast on a leather couch with a table for my own electronic gear, I logged onto my university site. There were the familiar fantasy projections of my students in all their digital finery, now affecting attention—undoubtedly having been alerted by some alarm to my return. That was fine . . . feigned attention is better than none at all, so I was able to take care of business fairly efficiently, and we all were more or less relieved to see the end of the semester hove into sight. Then the little avatars began to disperse . . . except for one that had been indistinctly ghosting on the edges of my group. Now it manifested more clearly—a strangely simple, smiling, malevolent cartoon character—and spoke.

"Very professional, Professor. Impressive academic use of the technology . . . well . . . gimmicky and not terribly sophisticated in terms of algorithms and all, but for the English Department, not bad."

Next to me, Celeste tensed. She had been half-watching me work in case something dubious turned up. It seemed that something had. She put her ear against my headset to listen.

The avatar continued, "We know you are out of the city . . . it looks like middle Oregon. We'll have you fixed in a couple more minutes. Now why would a professor leave town at this point in the semester—the mobility of distance education notwithstanding? Seems at least an even bet you're off with Ms. Lathke on a wee adventure."

One thing about VR technologies is that while you can hide behind a facade, the responses, or lack of responses come across in a very realistic fashion.

Just as Celeste hissed, "It's them!" he continued, "Ah, your hesitation betrays you. You're really not cut out for cloak and dagger stuff, Professor. You will have figured out—with her help no doubt—who I am. Let's use her charming sobriquet for me, Maurice, shall we? He whom she so seriously underestimates, alas for her and those close to her."

This statement was delivered in the calmest of tones, almost completely uninflected or colored by emotion. It was so benign-sounding that it was very disturbing.

"What do you want? And why are you lurking in my course?"

"Ah, those are questions you already have the answers to . . . so professorial, so rhetorical. I am here—here, ha! Wherever that may be—to pass a message to your partner in crime about her ailing father. Isn't that thoughtful of us?"

Celeste pulled frantically at my headset, trying to get into a position to speak into the microphone, saying, "What have you done to my father, you bastard? If you have . . ."

But the avatar was even then pixelating and dissolving, the smiling face the last to go, a hideous spoof on the Cheshire Cat.

Celeste threw the VR set to the floor in fury, drawing alarmed stares from other patrons.

"I've got to get back! I should never have left him. I just couldn't believe they would go that far."

"But what will you do? How will you—"

"Listen, Charles, I'm going back. But you must keep going—disappear for a while, protect the bloody book."

"No, I'll take you."

"No!" She'd lowered her voice, but it was still ferocious.

"Maybe we should just destroy the damn thing."

She calmed somewhat at that but quite determinedly said, "Charles, please do as I ask. I have to go help my father, but they are just trying to get the book, and we both know it is precious. Look, I can take public transportation back. They'll be watching the airport, but if I don't have the book, and don't know where it is, they'll see the futility of the threat."

I tried to offer other ideas, but that ferociousness returned. She was suddenly single-minded, all the personable traits I had begun to enjoy were now subsumed in this warrior persona. It was more than a daughter's concern for her father. She seemed almost to have forgotten me, certainly as an equal partner. Frankly, I found this complete personality change alarming. This was undoubtedly the Celeste Lathke who had been fighting the geek thugs for years single-handedly, the woman who had broken into my system, my home, and stolen from me. I realized with fresh insight who had dragged me into this weird and dangerous adventure . . . along with her dad. *A curse on the Lathkes*, I thought. All at once, we were miles apart, on our own, and that lovely framework of communication, of communion even, was demolished.

I hastily turned off my equipment, and we roared off north to the relatively large, thus somewhat more anonymous city of Portland, where a few hours later, we parted.

The last thing she said was, "Memorize this and contact me in a week . . . not sooner!"

No hug or kiss on the cheek, no expression for my own safety, just a woman running into an airport with catlike deadly grace.

Back at the car, I sat stunned. I looked at the paper; it was a generic email address.

TEN

Aimless is a good word. It connotes more—or is it less?—than the lack of a goal or target. With no target, there can be no aiming of the arrow, not even the beginning of purposeful action. Thus, in Portland after seeing Celeste off, I wandered aimlessly. Randomly, I stopped, lost on a leafy street. Across the way was an anachronistic building, and with my fondness for anachronism, I parked, grabbed my small pack containing my electronics and the book, and walked over to it.

Rising like a stony promontory through the trees were crenelated walls, a stolid tower, gothic windows, and a brilliant-red door flung wide. There was a barely perceptible golden hue glowing faintly within the portals that drew me like the smell of savory cooking into the church. As I stepped into the foyer, I heard, too, the sound of music, that old-fashioned music one hears almost exclusively these days in Episcopal churches, the music of the likes of Handel or Telemann. Drawn further by the increasing golden light and swelling music, I glided into a most beautiful sanctuary . . . and this, too, it seemed in its original sense of the word.

In a perfect demonstration of visual perspective, the gold-lit room swept back, a receding triangle punctuated above by great A-shaped beams of delicate tracery that would have seemed overly ornate had they not been of huge black limbs of wood perfectly crafted to soar in easy defiance of gravity. Blue stained glass windows accented the walls like sapphires in a golden ring. And all pointed to the blaze of fiery-yellow vault and the diamond-like round window held aloft in the sublime setting of wood-encased organ pipes, below which the altar seemed a modest understatement.

I sat toward the right rear to maintain the sense of perspective and not disturb the practicing choir, which started and stopped, polishing small sections of music, like a jeweler polishing various facets of a gem. This prosaic craftsmanship added to the warmth of the scene and harmonized all into a homey comfort. I then remembered another time I had come into a cathedral midweek and heard sacred music being practiced. It was in Chartres. The huge organ was mounted high up on one wall of the cavernous interior, clinging darkly like an immense bat on a high cliff. The music, too, was colossal, and when the player—tiny in his aerie—depressed the foot pedals, the bass notes detonated in a way that surpassed sound; the very stones of the building above and below shook and thundered. That church was the house of an Old Testament God, unimaginably mighty, and mere mortals came into His presence on their knees and in fearful supplication. This Portland church was a New Testament church, a place of human scale, still grand and majestic, but welcoming to and encouraging of other sensibilities, a place where the meek might indeed feel exalted.

I tried not to think too much about my situation, about Celeste and the rest, but the mind is rarely subject to the bridle, and I began to wonder about the book. I'd not opened it since the campground, and that seemed long ago. I retrieved it from my pack, saw a simple gold design on the otherwise blank cover and opened it. Always surprised by the thing, I was surprised anew to find it to be a hymnal . . . appropriately Episcopal.

I thumbed the pages and deep into it saw the old song "This Is My Father's World," which bounced me as sure as a well-struck golf ball into childhood and the boys choir I sang in at the community church my agnostic parents thought I should be exposed to. While I was not then cognizant of the presence of the Father the song mentions, I was nonetheless quite taken with the singing of nature, all those rocks and trees and especially the music of the spheres. It was surely the first time I encountered the phrase or the idea of singing spheres. Was it planets? Singing? With the rocks and trees? It was a theology I could almost grasp and perhaps my first experience of the power of metaphor. So while it failed to render in me the spiritual faith as intended, which might've led to some Christian vocation, it did render me open to the lesser vocation of lover of literature and believer in its power, a faith to which I still cleaved, the inadequacies of my profession notwithstanding.

Deep in these thoughts, I was unaware that anyone had approached until a mocking voice said from the pew just behind me, "Really, Professor, you surprise me."

I lurched as if coming awake and turned to see none other than Maurice behind and to the left of me, leaning forward with his elbows on the back of the pew I was in. I was speechless.

He smiled and said casually, "You really have no feel for this, do you? I mean, here you are sitting in a church, what? Praying for guidance? You've got your electronics incompletely turned off, and as we had already had you first thing this morning in Oregon, I popped up to Portland on the corporate jet, and you considerately came to me. It was child's play to find you here."

He held in his hand a small device, which must have had some capability to track my signals somehow still being emitted like tiny traitors from my gear. Putting it down, he reached over and began rummaging through my pack on the bench before him, saying, "I'll just relieve you of the book and be on my way."

But the book was not there; it was lying open on my lap with the music of the spheres singing softly from its pages. Maurice looked around, saw the other hymnals in the racks on the seat back, took in my identical-looking one, and was himself speechless for a moment.

"You don't have it? She took it back with her? You are stupider than I thought!"

With that, he bolted from the pew and right out the door. I watched him go and realized I had not spoken a word to him. I looked back down at the book and read, "The birds their carols raise, the morning light, the lily white, declare their Maker's praise," and found myself having to agree.

I rose and began walking slowly toward the exit, stuffing the book into my pack, briefly worried that a priest or someone might think I was stealing a hymnal. But I comforted myself with the thought that surely he or she would remember the road to Emmaus and think, *Take my cloak also.*

None the wiser myself, though, I was rather thinking of another biblical road story: the road to Damascus where Paul was knocked senseless off his horse but was given understanding by way of compensation. No such luck for me as I slid back into my car.

One thing I did realize, though, was that with the geek thugs sure I didn't have the book, certain, too, I was too lame to hide from them if I had, they had for the time being written me out of the story. I was in this regard free, for a time anyway. There was at the moment no reason to bother trying to stay electronically dark. But I still had nowhere to go, nothing much to do, no way I could help Celeste . . . not sure I even wanted to for that matter. I had a little bit of work to do in closing out the semester, which I could do at my leisure. And here I was in Portland. Looking at a map, I saw I was not far from some places I'd heard of but not been, like Mount Hood, so on a whim, I headed out on Highway 84 along the scenic Hood River.

After all this adventure, I was now just a tourist. I stopped at Multnomah Falls, drawn like any tourist to its majesty and the breathtakingly picturesque bridge that arched halfway up the cliff, seeming to bisect the thundering, white spring cataract. I walked up the inviting paved trail that was surprisingly empty, realizing that I had, through dumb luck, arrived before schools had gotten out and thus before most visitors. The bridge drew me across, though it was veiled in swirling mist, itself blown by the wind made by the tons and tons of falling water, water moving faster than gravity alone seemed capable of causing. The percussive, tearing din added to the feeling that the whole world was shaking, while I alone on the little bridge, vacillated between cowering and exultation. It was the setting of a fairy tale, and I half-expected some otherworldly being to appear from the swirling gray mist. Instead, a blast of wind threw a torrent of heavy drops into my face, and I ran for the relatively protected rock face beyond the end of the bridge.

The feeling of incipient magic remained, and I saw that the trail continued up an increasingly steep incline. *This must be,* I thought, *where the thousands of corpulent day-trippers turn around.* Within this little moment of pride, I felt a burning sensation slowly but steadily make itself felt in my legs. *Hmm, okay then,* I thought, *no more of that.* And on up I went, stopping now and then to take in the increasingly stunning vistas of the river valley as they were sporadically and generously revealed by switchbacks, and also to rest.

Finally, the trail left the cliff face and crested the hill, turning inland into the forest. The ferocious sound of the falls was ever present but somewhat muted by the trees. Then the trail came out to a stream, full and lively, but not one that one would expect to be associated with such a grand waterfall. So I was off guard when, on rounding a small turn in the trail, I found myself just feet away from a place where the stone bottom of the stream fell out from supporting the water, which kept going, pouring clearly out into the air, turning white, ripping into torrents and tendrils, and sailing into a void below which no bottom could be seen, only space and, far off, a distant forest ceiling. I felt like there was suddenly an increase of gravity, as if it had swirled in a powerful vortex pulling the water—the very stream bed into space . . . and if I were not careful I would get sucked over too. I fought off the rising dizziness and retreated to a safer vantage point, sat on a fallen log worn smooth by the bottoms of many a similarly woozy hiker, and watched the endlessly shifting gouts of water being jettisoned from the edge of the world.

On the way down, legs burning, I wondered what Maurice would have made of the spectacle. Would he have been awed? Would it be possible for any human being not to be? I realized that I didn't really understand the modern city dweller not of my generation. Do they simply not know that such places exist? Do they not see the majesty, feel the power, indeed respond to the muse-like inspiration of what I have long called Big Nature? Somehow VR and all that busy communication of shallow inanities in the techno world failed to measure up to one really good waterfall, one swirling mist cloud that seemed to me to suggest dozens of stories of things, beings, and ideas beyond the normal ken of all the sophisticated Maurices of the day. These thoughts—probably of a variety considered by every graying generation in the history of the world—did not, could not persist. I was descending through a forest on the edge of a precipice, now in view of vast distances, now surrounded by mossy tree boles, and always within the reverberation of the mighty waterfall. And that was more than enough.

Deafened, stunned, and cleansed, I drove on until I arrived at the nearly deserted Mount Hood Lodge, still partially blanketed by snow.

I ascended the front steps to the fortress-like stone entrance, the side of which was clutched by a rampart of sculpted snow. The keystone above the arching doorway was as big as a car. Immediately I saw that all pieces of hardware, from door pull to hinges to massive interior gates, were unique, individual, artistic creations crafted by forge, anvil, and hammer in heavy iron. I realized that this, too, was a building of a past time. It was surely built by the WPA, one of dozens of Depression-era projects that put millions to work throwing bridges over streams and making stone lodges in national parks across the country. The attention to detail was astonishing. The workers had nowhere else to go, nothing other to do, so they performed each task as if it was to be their personal legacy to the world. The massive, multisided stone fireplace and chimney soared to the high ceiling in the center of the round main room. An encircling balcony built of immense beams from first-growth forests looked down on the cozy couches and nooks; a post at the bottom of a staircase started at the floor as a rough fir log and ended as a carved eagle; panels of carved western-immigration scenes and intricate, weighty wrought iron furnishings abounded in the woody light of the smoke-dusted fireplace.

Here, too, was another kind of cathedral, one dedicated to nature, the massive stones harmonizing with those of the mountain, the tree trunk beams mirroring those of the forest below, while carvings throughout paid homage to the wildlife beyond. For all that, it was, like the church in Portland, of human scale . . . or nearly so. It was more grand and noble than most of us are, but not so grand that we cannot imagine that we at our best might rise to fit such a setting, ennobled by the marriage of nature and human imagination.

I got a room, telling the soft-spoken young woman that I didn't know how long I would want to stay. She smiled a smile that told me it was not the first time she had heard the statement, knowing the place and the stunning mountain out the windows was quick to weave a spell. I was again lucky that I preceded the summer hordes and was thereby free to linger.

It was by the window overlooking the snowy peak that I later found myself sipping one of the dozens of microbrews from the area with their funny names and rich flavors. For a while, I was content to ponder, but halfway into my second ale—a different one chosen for the unfamiliar name alone—I remembered my last contemplative moment that had been so startlingly interrupted by Maurice. I looked around in the cozy light as the last of the gloaming tinted the window orange, and saw—and believed—I was alone. I got the book out, thinking that if it were true, as Celeste maintained, that the book could somehow reflect or guide . . . or something . . . the reader, then surely this was a good time to see what it had to say.

I opened the now nondescript cover and found the pages . . . blank. What a shock. There was not a single word on any page—I checked each one. I remembered what Celeste's father had said about finding it blank and thinking it a presentiment of death. I felt a surge of anger. This damned thing was not going to do that to me. I didn't even believe in it. It was not going to rule me the way it ruled those other crazies (I included Celeste in this condemnation). I would take control. I rifled my daypack for a pen (yes, of course it was a fountain pen. It should come as no surprise!). I whipped the pages back to the first blank one and began to write furiously.

Celeste hurried out of the airport with an intensity double that of a businessman late for the meeting of his life. She was certain that Ray's arrogance would manifest in his sending a liveried driver to await her arrival with a card on which her name was printed in calligraphy. But there was no one there, and she realized that his arrogance was calibrated yet higher: he knew he had her running to him in fevered capitulation, and he would make her come the rest of the way on her own via taxi in which she could further worry about her father. This was indeed how she arrived at the hip restored loft in which his software empire spun its webs. The interior was, as so many computer businesses have been for years, designed for the extended adolescence of the geniuses who come straight from college frat houses to their six-figure incomes, all skateboards and basketball courts and haphazard couches and techno gadgets.

She blew past the caricature receptionist straight into Ray's corner-office domain, where he stood up in quickly concealed alarm.

"Where is he?" she demanded.

"He?"

"You know, you ass, my father."

"I assume your dear old dad is at home or in his quaint shop. But why do you ask me?"

"You know damn well why! You and Maurice are trying to get the book by threatening my father."

"Really, Celeste, I do love your passion . . . I remember it quite well in fact . . ."

She squinted at his leer with disgust. "My father—"

"He's fine," Ray conceded. "Here, let's call him. I have his number right here."

He pushed a button on his console, and in a moment, they heard Mr. Lathke's tentative, "Hello, Lathke Stringed Instruments."

"Daddy?"

"Celeste? Where are you? Are you all right? Those men—"

"Yes, yes, I'm fine. Are you okay? Did they threaten you or hurt you in any way?"

"I'm fine. They didn't really do anything, just asked for you and... well, I had nothing to tell them. What's—"

"Listen, Daddy, I have to go. I just wanted to check, but I'll talk to you soon."

Ray disconnected the call, smiling benignly. "You see? We didn't do anything to 'Daddy,' just wanted to get your attention, help you focus a bit on what's important."

"Ray, you are such an ass."

"You've expressed that opinion before."

"Do you think this is a game?"

He raised his eyebrows and said with mock sincerity, "Do you think it isn't a game? We just decided to raise the ante a little."

Suddenly, she sprang around the desk and, catching him completely unprepared, crashed her forearms into his chest, driving him forcefully back into the glass picture window. His head snapped back, striking the glass so hard it seemed that surely the glass would shatter and both would tumble out onto the sidewalk far below. She pinned him there while his swimming brain cleared.

Then she whispered fiercely, "I'm upping the ante too, asshole. You so much as go near my father again and I will kill you. No little computer simulation. Hell with the consequences. Am I being clear? Do you understand me? Do you get how bloody serious I am right now, gamer?"

Ray was deeply surprised and shaken. She had been right to call him a gamer, a guy who shoots and kills only in the virtual world, and this very real, physical expression of violence stunned him. He just looked at her, trying to process the escalation of their conflict. His machine announced an incoming call, and Celeste let him go to push the answer button.

Trying with limited success to regain his sense of confidence, he answered, "Yeah, what's going on? You get it?"

The voice over the speaker was Maurice's. "The professor doesn't have it."

Ray looked up at Celeste, who had an expression of wary concern.

"What? He's gotta have it. You sure you . . . ?"

"Yeah, I checked . . . caught him in Portland . . . clueless . . . went through his stuff—backpack, car. He doesn't have it . . . unless he buried it, which I'm sure he didn't. He thought he was unfindable, invisible. The guy's an idiot. He doesn't have the bleedin' thing. Must be on Celeste. She there yet?"

"She's standing right here. Get your ass back here." Without waiting for a reply, he hung up. Celeste had an unreadable look on her face. She pointed at the window. He turned and saw with dismay the crack that was traversing the window. When he turned back, the door was closing behind Celeste, and he looked back at the window, for the moment humbled.

Celeste left the building also confused. *What*, she wondered, *happened in Portland? What did Charles do with the book?* She knew better than to try to contact him.

Hailing a cab, she directed the driver on a circuitous path through San Francisco, finally arriving at Charles's apartment where, as before, seemingly a long time ago, she had similarly let herself in. There was some riesling in the fridge. She poured herself a glass and sat on the couch in the dimming light . . . stymied.

At least that's something like what I wrote . . . more or less. Well, yes, plus what I learned later from Celeste herself, so yeah, I am adding stuff here. I can't check the original, of course.

Like Celeste and Ray, I was deep in thought, staring into a fading fire in the great fireplace of the lodge. Next to an empty beer glass, the book lay open on the last page of the short piece I had just written. The orange embers heaving with occasional wands of blue and yellow flame looked like the remnants of an ancient city, sacked, burned, and collapsing . . . or perhaps going the other way, taking new form, phoenixlike. Mesmerized, I pondered how the book had appeared blank, allowing me to write the story. I picked it up, then slowly closed and reopened it. Again it was blank, expectant, as if waiting for an author to invent a story for it to hold, to transmit . . . and then erase.

I had an idea, a flicker of a plan, unfinished, like the inchoate structures in the fire. I needed to write it down, to see how the idea blossomed in the process of writing. But not in the book. I needed an older technology that I could control, contain. Quill and parchment would be ideal, but paper and pen would do. These I had, and in the quiet chrysalis of the orange-hued stone room, I began to compose . . . only half-sure where it was heading.

Lost once again in writing, I did not notice the passing of hours, the closing of bar and restaurant, the tiptoeing departure of staff. My mind was wholly taken up in the story I virtually (another word I use in its historic sense) saw unfolding before me. Such is the experience of the writer, to be an observer, a mere scribe recording events happening by actors for reasons beyond his ken.

And when I was finished, there was a hint of a newer version of orange in the windows replacing that which had long ago drained from the fireplace. My brain felt like steel wool, my tongue like a desiccated mummy. With my last wisp of coherence, I managed to send an innocuous message to a university colleague in another department requesting a meeting on . . . what day? No, not this one; this one was for sleeping. The day after . . . what's the word? Oh, *tomorrow*, I would come to his office late in the day.

It was with dull surprise on that next day that after a very long drive and a complicated discussion with my colleague about my idea, I at last opened the door to what had once been a sanctuary, my home, to see Celeste sleeping on the couch, empty wine glass at her elbow.

She stirred, opened her eyes, and said, "What's going on? Why are you back? Charles, what have you done with it?"

"Not now, Celeste," was all I could manage, and I went into the bedroom, closed the door firmly, as if to lock all of that—and her—out. The bed literally pulled me into it.

ELEVEN

Sometimes it is a blessing not to be able to remember one's dreams. All I knew when I woke the next morning was that my brain felt worn out, as if it had cycled through every possible permutation of a weird, anxious storyline. I marveled only at the mind's uncanny ability to fashion intricately detailed places, people, and interwoven events all in real time. How could that be?

And there was Celeste again, sitting at my table, drinking coffee. Her face was difficult to read, seeming a collage of hesitant familiarity, wary uncertainty, curiosity, and resignation. She seemed to know that the proverbial ball was not in her court. She waited for me to serve it up, but I only glanced her way and served myself coffee, which I must say had been well-made.

I went into the living room to sit on the couch but, remembering that it had been her bed, veered over to the chair. I think she saw it and guessed what had happened because she looked away when I raised my eyes.

The silence was heavy, hanging there between us like a curtain.

Finally, she said, "May I stay here for a while?"

"Must you?"

Her gaze dropped to her coffee. "They'll be looking for me again."

"I suppose you're right about that."

Her mouth tightened at the edges, and with effort she said, "I thought we . . ."

I looked over at her, seemingly from a great distance, and said, "Yes, I did too." I paused, trying to read those tawny eyes, and added, "But I understand that it might be a good place to hide for a short while."

"Not as good as Oregon."

"I don't know; they had no trouble finding me there, so maybe all that was just . . . fantasy."

It appeared that her eyes welled up a little, but she clearly had great control, and no tear fell. I still felt as if we were looking at each other across a gulf.

I did understand what we—I—had just done, and so I threw her a thin lifeline, saying, "Don't worry about the book for now. It's safe enough."

"Oh, okay . . . well, that's good."

I rose and walked back into the kitchen. "So anything in here to eat?"

"I hope so; I'm famished."

-

Later, Celeste turned toward me, her hands in the soapy water of the sink, and asked if I had plans for the day. She still had not broached the subject of the book, which I appreciated.

When I hesitated, she quickly added, "It's just that Daddy . . . my father . . . is planning on closing the shop after all these years. I was planning on going by to see if he wanted help, and since you know him and all . . ."

It was strange to see this new Celeste. She seemed to have lost her swift, confident manner, the feline surety. Something must have happened to shake her psychologically. I had guessed, even up there in the Mount Hood Lodge, but details, of course, were not yet clear to me. I wasn't sure I wanted them. Wouldn't they make me feel more responsible?

I said as kindly as I could, “Sure, I’ll go with you.” In response to her relieved expression, I added lightly, “I want to thank your old man for getting me involved in all this madness.”

She winced at that, and I hastened to add, “I needed a summertime hobby. Want to go soon?”

Within the hour, we passed through the shop door with its Closed sign, me hearing the nonexistent bell, and entered the old-world environment of wooden music.

Mr. Lathke hurried from the back and gave his daughter a quick hug before turning to me with an outstretched hand and an apologetic half smile on his face.

“Ah, Professor, it is good to see you. I fear I have rather embroiled you in a bit more drama than either of us was looking to.”

I shook his hand and, holding it longer than necessary, replied, “I do believe you are an excellent psychologist, among other skills, sir.”

“A dilettante?”

“In the old sense of the word, yes.”

“I thank you.”

We both smiled, remembering our first conversation. Celeste looked on bemusedly.

She said, “What can we help you with, Daddy? You’ve cleaned up a lot, but most of the instruments are still up on the walls.”

“Yes, I thought it best to leave them safely above the fray, which I am happy to say has nearly subsided. All the business aspects are tidied . . . surprisingly little there after all this time . . . most of which I simply threw away. No need to keep the records of a declining old shop with almost no taxable income or assets . . . almost no official . . . or lasting . . . footprint.” This last was spoken with the wistfulness the aging often express as they see each generation’s brave new world supplanting their own.

It was a fleeting moment, quickly covered with a cheery, "Just need to pack some of the instruments off to their various new homes."

"Where are they going?" Celeste asked.

"Oh, here and there . . . old friends, a few museums . . . and . . . well, this is as good a time as any."

He turned to the workbench where my guitar had been repaired. A small, battered instrument case was lying there. He picked it up gently, turned, and placed it in my hands.

"A small gift from one dilettante to another. No, do not protest. Please enjoy it and, as we once spoke of, its story."

I nodded, placed it on the bench, and opened it. Inside was a small antique instrument about the size of an ukelele but with a different array of strings. I ran my fingers across the strings. Reentrant tuning, like the ukelele, a high note below the bass notes.

"Very uke-like," I said.

"The ukelele's forebear, originally from Madeira, Portugal," he said, reaching into the case and retrieving a small, yellowed piece of paper.

He handed it to me, and on it I saw the words, which I read aloud with considerable surprise, "Rajão, Honolulu, Kingdom of Hawaii via *Ravenscrag*, 1879."

I looked at Celeste and saw the shot go home. The story we had read at Clear Lake. It was the first time we had made genuine eye contact since . . . when? That very camp site?

Thankfully, Mr. Lathke interrupted our incredulity. "And I have a gift for you as well, my dear. It is, in its way, something of a concession, an apology, if you wish."

He reached to the wall above the bench and brought down a beautiful instrument that was hanging on a peg.

"Daddy . . . a violin, oh . . ."

"No dear, look at the flattened bridge . . . a fiddle."

There were tears in her eyes as she placed it under her chin and brushed the strings with the fingers of her fretting hand. The instrument was obviously very resonant and already in perfect tune.

Mr. Lathke handed her a bow, saying, "What it lacks in pedigree it makes up for in age."

Celeste closed her eyes, one small tear escaping down her cheek, and without warm-up or prelude, played a lightning-fast jig—perfectly. I was floored and glanced quickly over to her father, who even then was handing me a guitar from the wall, taking the rajão. Celeste sensed the movement, took in the exchange, and smoothly changed rhythm into slow three-quarter time, and I immediately recognized the gorgeous tune by O'Carolan. I put my foot up on a stool, timed my entry, and joined in. Instantly we were swept away by the timeless melody.

Mr. Lathke's eyes were shining when we finished, but surprisingly he was quick to break the spell by announcing that he wanted to discuss the disposition of the building upstairs with Celeste.

"Upstairs?" I asked.

"The apartment. Very old-fashioned, apartment above the shop, yes?"

Once again, I was politely if rather hastily escorted to the door, seeing Celeste hang back with a sad smile on her face. And once again, I was standing outside the old atelier looking at my reflection in the glass door. Would Celeste return to my place or stay here in the apartment or what? What did I prefer? "Ah, well," I told myself, "perhaps it would indeed be best if she stayed away. Such an intense woman. Besides, I do need at least a week for my little plan to germinate." I sauntered home in feigned nonchalance, whistling the O'Carolan piece.

TWELVE

Celeste did stay away, and at times I missed her quite a bit. At other times, though, I was more than content to return to my more solitary existence. I had friends, after all, colleagues and otherwise with whom I socialized. In addition to getting a break from the craziness of the whole geek-thugs-out-to-take-over-the-world thing, I began to enter into that sweet amnesia that many of us in my profession succumb to each summer. Job? What job? It is a time of relaxation, of travel, writing, reflection . . . a blessed holdover from another age . . . summer vacation. Oh, yes, with the advent of online, distance-education courses, timing really didn't matter anymore. Still, my college clung to the archaic order of semesters the way earlier schools had kept Easter break, which had utterly morphed in purpose—once a time of religious duties and observation, then the bacchanal of spring break.

I did meet several more times with my college colleague about our little secret project we had begun after my return from Oregon, but that was actually fun, intellectually challenging, creative even. We sat over coffee in a sun-dappled sidewalk café and chatted like any two friends. Oh, yes, I did have the sense that the geeks were keeping loose watch over me, casually monitoring my computer and movements. *Let them*, I thought.

I didn't open the book once. It sat, again hidden in plain sight on my bookcase. For all I knew it was still shooting blanks.

Not only did I not see her in that time, never once did I even hear from Celeste, and I told myself that that, too, was fine by me—considering how she would surely react to the plan . . . though at times that haunting Irish music was in my head for hours.

As for the other musical aspect, that little rajão that Mr. Lathke had given me, I had almost willfully forgotten it. That is, I had purposely tucked it away where it would be safe, and so it was out of mind as well. But it did eventually resurface, especially with the O'Carolan music to remind me. When I took it again from the case, the little note of its provenance slipped out, and opening it, I involuntarily flinched back. As much as I had retreated from the whole crazy magic book thing, its mystery was again here before me. I, of course, couldn't go back into the book to the little girl's story to check the name of the ship and date, as they were long since erased from its pages, but in my reasonably clear memory, they were the same. And if so, what? How could that be explained? The instrument and the story. Connected how? They came from the same family, the same man, really. Mr. Lathke gave me both. Both came from the instrument shop. But so what? Was the little, old-world dilettante sitting in his dark atelier collecting and building instruments and somehow inventing stories to go with them and then inserting them in the book? It was too much of a fairy tale to believe. *It would, though,* I thought, *make a nice fairy tale.* Maybe one day I would write it. Thus, in circles did I think.

I then realized that all this thinking was preventing me from actually playing the little instrument. So I strummed it. It had a surprising sound, something quite like the ukelele but brightly distinctive as well. I assumed that Mr. Lathke had tuned the six strings properly. Like the uke, the upper string—what would be the low E on a guitar—was an octave higher than one might expect. Unlike the uke, though, the next string was also higher. Then it dropped down an octave and was predictably rising in pitch as the strum went down the strings . . .

except that the last note was sounded by two strings set quite close to each other. One further thing gave it a different voice than the uke: the strings were steel, so the sound was sparkling, airy, and ringing.

But this was still not really playing it. Having a passing knowledge of some ukelele chords, I was quickly able to suss out fingering for a number on the rajão. And soon I was playing music—chords, linking runs, and figures. Not, surely, that of its native Madeira Island, but pretty stuff of my own—somewhat halting—invention. It is a strange thing when one clicks into this kind of playing. There is almost a physical sensation of the left brain relinquishing control to the more emotive, less wordy right. It is slightly intoxicating. Certainly, the sense of the passing of time (temporal not rhythmic) is suspended. Thus, I seemed to more listen to than play music, which rang like tiny bells in a miniature carillon.

Later, the clock told me I had been in the land of faery for nearly an hour. An enchanted hour, I thought. The gentle power of art.

-

I was more or less slapped awake a few days later on reading a news piece about a highly touted tech company, ApolloNet—with its disconcerting logo of Apollo's chariot pulling a microprocessor sun—being given an extraordinary government contract to network and control the entire country's electrical grid. I realized that it was the geek thugs' company. Not only did they now control most of the wireless communication technology for the country—thus, much of the world—they now were being given control of the main power switch.

I made a couple of calls, one of which was to a skeptical executive assistant who, on checking with her boss, hastily gave me an appointment for the following day. I also sent a message to Celeste—not wanting her to quiz me in a direct conversation—inviting her to join me. This gave me a jolt of nervousness. It couldn't be helped, I reassured myself.

But the nervousness was compounded as she came into the waiting room and sat down warily. The silence was very thick between us. Then we were ushered together into Ray's office. Ray was standing behind his desk, also looking wary . . . at Celeste. Near him was a large man who reeked of "security," and who glanced from Ray to Celeste and then quickly at a surprising crack in the glass behind Ray. Of course, the arrogant Maurice was there as well, VR headset and glove on, engaged in something.

We all sat. There was no attempt at greeting or the small talk that typically lubricates the transition to business. Without it, we all seemed hesitant.

Ray looked at Maurice and said, "Get off that thing."

Maurice didn't hear him, so Ray made some gesture on his console, and Maurice shouted, "Hey!" wrenching his headset off.

I looked from him to Ray and asked, "You can shock people through their headsets?"

He smiled and replied, "A new wrinkle we're playing with . . . everything's electric, you know . . . I should think a professor would love it for inattentive students . . . like Maurice here."

Now Maurice was impatient and said, "Well?"

I had a neat little speech prepared, but it evaporated when I glanced at Celeste. I opened the pack that was on the floor, the same one Maurice had rifled—I could see he recognized it. I stood, walked over to the front of Ray's desk, pointedly bypassing Maurice, and reached into the bag. This made the security guy flex for potential action.

I said to Ray, "You win already. Leave us alone."

I pulled the book in my hand out of the bag and spun it onto the desk.

Celeste shrieked, "Charles! No!" and tried to run over to grab the book.

Ray swept the book up and flinched back against the glass, then quickly flinched away from it too. The security guy intercepted her, and she spun toward me and punched me right in the jaw. I went down seeing stars.

When I sat up on the carpet, it seemed decorum had been reestablished. Celeste was sitting again below the towering guard, fury and betrayed outrage lasering at me. Maurice and Ray were triumphant, huddled almost reverently over the cover of the book in Ray's hands.

Then Ray looked up, saw that we were accounted for and tame, and pulled the book from under Maurice's gaze, which earned a frown and a sharp look of . . . something . . . competition?

Ray settled in his chair in a lordly fashion, saying, "All right, boys and girls—girl, that is—schoolyard restored to order? How about a little story before nap time."

Celeste sputtered at this condescension but resignedly leaned back in her chair. I rose, rubbing my jaw, and, avoiding looking at Celeste, went to another chair.

Ray opened the book and read.

White Horses of the Celtic Sea-God

Brilliant in our wake stood the mysterious, silver pillar that rises from the deep. On we old companions sailed toward the setting sun, as the sea-god, Manannán mac Lir, had pointed us when we met at sea—he in his chariot, *Ocean Sweeper*, pulled by the great white mare. Two more days and nights on a smooth gray sea, hardly a horse's mane to be seen, only moonlight streaking the water. Then a pale-green shore rose on the horizon before us with a broad bay at its heart. Into this we sailed, thinking we had finally found the western lands of legend after the long weeks of sailing since we left our war-ravaged homeland.

The bay narrowed sharply as we entered, and we could see a wide green river that emptied at its center, almost a replica in inviting shape. Along the placid riverbanks were bright fruit trees, which reminded us of the strange, lulling music of the apple branch from Emain Albach, the inspiration of our journey. But our progress was halted by the powerful current against which we strove. It was not the gentle flow of the river but the tide drawing out of the bay, and we were obliged to anchor and wait for it to go slack before venturing farther.

The sandy berm; the pluming azure waves, which rose out of the smooth sea to break on either hand; and the shimmering, tree-lined river marked the land as blessed as one of Brighid's own.

At slack tide, we rowed up into the river valley. The silvery water reflected the laden fruit trees, so it seemed for a time that we were gliding like birds over the treetops. The river curved in gentle bends, each opening upon a fresh prospect of trees and meadows and wooded slopes beyond. Thus, for an hour or more we rowed, while the valley and its river grew gradually more and more narrow, finally becoming little more than a spear's throw from bank to bank. Then, at the end of a sweeping curve, on a low gray bluff we saw a magnificent white fortress bright with sun.

Mounting the rise on foot, we passed through a columned portico and entered a resplendent hall through doors flung wide. The place was empty except for a sumptuous banquet laid out before richly brocaded chairs equaling our exact number. Hostless, we nevertheless determined the feast to be in our honor, and we sat and ate our fill, drinking, too, the heady brown ale that filled silver goblets before us. Marveling and laughing, we delighted in our good fortune.

Before long, however, we bethought to continue on our way. Happy enough to eat in that strange place, we were loath to sleep there, and so took with us such food and drink we had not consumed. One sailor, seeing nothing to prevent him, dared secret one of the great goblets in his shirt as a token or trophy of the feast. So we wound our way down from the quiet hall to the shiny river and our boats.

Suddenly, we heard a deafening roar, of land or beast we could not tell. The terrible noise echoed up the river valley from the sea. And then we saw a marvel. Around a bend in the river swept a great bluish wave, the tide returning in a bore, gushing up the river, breaking into frothy manes at both shores, sweeping the bases of the trees. Borne upon the crest of this surge was a narrow boat, white foam billowing from its jaws, and steered by just one fierce man. With one hand he held fast the tiller, in the other he brandished a silver-tipped lance. And his voice bellowed and mixed with the din of the wave's passage to make the roaring that had frozen us to the bank, some with one foot raised to board our boat.

Approaching at terrible speed in midstream, the dreadful apparition neared, then suddenly, almost abreast of us, turned across the wave at an angle. With a sharp flick of his steering hand, he threw a lash over the tiller to bind the craft on course. Then, with amazing agility—for surely, his long beard hid a youthful face—he leaped forward toward the bow and then up onto the very joining board above the prow and cutwater. Both hands raised in fury, his toes like mighty fists gripping over the gunnel, he rode—nay, flew—across the wall of water. Suddenly, he reared back and hurled the lance into our cowering midst. It flew like a splinter of silver lightning right through the man who had stolen the goblet, who threw his hands and then soul to the wind and crumbled as if burned into a pile of gray ashes, the goblet rolling right to my own feet.

Then the wave, the boat, and the terrible warrior were on us at once. He leaped ashore and seized the goblet just as the water splashed to our knees. He raised the goblet and drank, for it was suddenly full again of brown ale, and we knew then that he was the castellan of the great hall. With his fierce face no farther than a span from mine, he held my gaze unblinking, then turned and strode up to his white fortress.

Hurriedly emptying our swamped boats, we hastened to depart. But now our progress was again hindered, for the tidal surge had caused the river waters to flow upstream. So we were forced to row against it down to the safety of the open sea. All the while our thoughts were behind, rehearsing the wonders we had seen, and below breath, each gray-haired man whispered of the wonders of Brighid's isles, where the world was being remade.

Clearly it was not the story either Ray or Maurice expected. They probably thought it would be a futuristic piece more obviously about the brave new world they were ushering in. Celeste, too, when I hazarded a glance, looked puzzled.

Maurice was first to attempt speech but fizzled after, "What the . . ."

After a long silence, Ray turned to me and asked, "What do you make of it?"

I replied, "How would I know? It's your story. Isn't the book supposed to make stories that fit the reader?"

"Yeah, that's the idea as I understand it, but . . . you're the lit guy. What's it mean?"

I shrugged. "Well, there may be some other influences because of the variety of people in the room. Celeste?"

She glowered and said, "I pass."

Ray slammed the book closed, which made us all flinch. He reopened it, and there was, as usual, another story waiting. In frustration, he slammed it shut again and said, "We just need to figure out the first one. That's the important one. Do your interpretation schtick, Professor."

"Well," I started, "you certainly made it a lot harder by erasing the story so we can't refer to it. Nice job so far, Ray, top marks."

His eyes went tight and dangerous, so I started running a pretty standard literary analysis. "Well, for starters, I can tell you that I recognize the context. The reference to the sea-god Manannán mac Lir in his chariot boat, *Ocean Sweeper*, comes straight out of Celtic mythology. So, too, does Brighid, Bride the Beautiful, Goddess of Western Shores, who interestingly evolved into Saint Bride of Ireland. And the Western Isles, too, that's Celtic myth. There are a number of sailing legends: Bran Mac Febal, Mael Duin, and of course Saint Brendan the Navigator, whose firsthand account is extant. All are part of a persistent idea that the Celts sailed northwest, island hopping all the way to the North American continent—centuries before the Vikings, let alone Columbus."

I stopped. "Am I boring you with this historical disquisition?"

Maurice barked, "Of course you are. You remind me why I hated lit classes and all this pompous mumbo jumbo."

"Mumbo jumbo, it may seem, but it is the mumbo jumbo of an ancient culture that is the foundation of our own, so it is not such a waste of time, I, in my pomposity, believe. Besides, I didn't bring it up. It's your story—your book. I don't give a bloody damn what it means! Figure it out yourself, hotshot."

I made to rise but was cut short by Ray's firm voice. "Sit down, Professor. Maurice, shut the hell up." When we had resettled, he added, "Pray continue your . . . what was it? Disquisition, yes, do, if you please."

Into this breach I plunged. "So these legends all concern sailing adventures where those guys I mentioned sail out with companions in boats called curraghs into the Atlantic where they encounter mythical stuff, like one enigmatic island that is peopled by a folk who laugh continually. When one of Bran's men goes ashore to ask why, he, too, dissolves into laughter, only to forget why when he reboards the boat. The sailors—and readers—never do learn the reason. And that silver pillar in the ocean in this story of yours; that's how they described icebergs. Eventually they come to an island called Emhain, as mentioned in the story. In English it's the Isle of Apples or Avalon, a name you might recognize from the King Arthur stories . . . or maps . . . as the Brits named a bunch of places that because of the importance of these myths."

I shot Maurice a look and continued, "This Isle of Apples, Avalon, is incidentally an island full of beautiful women where sadness and tiredness are unknown, a land of immortality. In Bran's story, homesick, they return home from this bountiful land, and they call to people along the shore only to learn that they have been away for generations, and they are remembered only in legend. One man, desperate to see his family, ventures onto the beach and immediately ages, then crumbles to dust. Seeing this, Bran lingers in Irish waters just long enough to write out his adventures on some wooden sticks in an ancient script called ogham. These he tosses to their descendants on shore before disappearing again over the western horizon.

"That crumbling-to-dust thing is like the guy getting killed in your story. So the Western Isles, then, represent the hopes of a wonderfully . . . even magically . . . better future of the people back in the east for whom life is a struggle. And here we are, all contextualized and back to your little tale. Now all we—you actually would be better suited in the sense that it comes somehow from you, or whatever the crazy book does—need to decide what the various events and images mean."

Maurice was beside himself. "All that, and we're ready to start? This is crazy."

"You're the ones who went to all this trouble to get the book. Well, now you have it. Use that much-vaunted brain power to figure out what the story means. Take it apart. I'll chime in if I have an insight. Celeste, too, is quite good at this sort of thing. It's right up her alley."

She continued to glower.

Maurice again made to protest, but Ray harshly cut him off. "Don't be such a baby, Maurice. We need to figure this out. If we know anything"—he shot a look at Celeste—"it's that this thing generates stories that are somehow directly beneficial to the reader. It doesn't matter that we don't know how it does it; it just seems to work, period. We just saw it generate two stories. It's in our possession . . . finally, so let's see if it's giving us a clue to our next moves."

Stung, Maurice muttered, "Next we'll be going to a freakin' fortune teller. Whatever . . . Why would it be written like that anyway? All old-fashioned with big, flowery words? No one talks like that. We sure don't, so what's it got to do with us?"

"Good question, Maurice," I said. "Language differences between time periods can be telling, and we could talk about why the archaic language is so, uh, difficult for younger generations."

"I never want to hear that old crap again; the sooner we finish getting rid of all that muck, the better. Why even have words that are confusing?"

"Why indeed. The old argument is that having a large vocabulary allows for more nuanced communication, but I concede your point: at times it can be a means of obfuscation."

"Wha . . . ?"

Ray interjected, "So, Professor, events and images, huh?"

I nodded.

"Like, um, well, the goblet for sure is important . . . and the castle owner guy . . ."

"Castellan," I added.

"Okay, him . . . and he's young and nimble . . . as opposed to the other dudes who it said were old gray hairs."

Maurice, recovering, chimed in, "And the castle man has this cool castle and can make pretty bitchin' beer magically fill that goblet . . . so maybe it's magic . . . or he is."

"Or both."

"Yeah, and he can provide the big feast for all those guys . . . just the right amount for their number . . . in an empty hall, no less."

They were getting into it now—and I thought briefly of the pleasures of talking about literature . . . even to these guys.

"And the wave and his boat . . ."

"Oh, and check it out, his boat goes on the wave . . . no oars like the other guys' boat . . ."

"Superior technology."

"Right, the new technology the young guy has is better than the old guys' technology."

Now they were starting to see some parallels to their own thoughts and situation, which made them more animated.

"Dude, it's like a VR game, the way the guy drives the boat and throws the spear from the front right through the goblet thief guy!"

"Scoring major points, man!"

"Oh, totally, and it's like he has harnessed nature—has it controlled."

"He has power . . . all the power."

"Right, and the island is totally the best place the guys have ever been—the best castle and an overflowing feast . . . it's his place."

"Hey, what was the last thing it said? You were stupid to close the book; we could've just looked."

I quoted the last phrase, "Where the world was being remade."

They looked at me and then each other. Ray whispered, "Like us."

"Yeah, and he's driving a chariot, like our ApolloNet logo!"

"See? You guys are already into ancient mythology. That logo fits perfectly . . . Apollo towing the sun across the sky, but as you suggest in the logo, the new sun is the microchip."

Suddenly, Celeste was at the door, turning haughtily and sweeping us all with one dark look. Slipping out, she said enigmatically, "Watch that window, Ray; you could get hurt."

It took a bit longer for me to get away from the newly minted literary enthusiasts, but eventually I did, rather wishing I'd had as much success with some of my students during the last semester.

THIRTEEN

"How do you even get in here, anyway? Do you have a key or what? And you really need to start contributing to the wine stock around here."

All of which Celeste ignored. She was leaning against my kitchen counter, draining the end of a glass of wine in the bright kitchen light, still with catlike grace, but tense. I held the bottle up to the light and saw a couple of inches left, so I grabbed a juice glass from the dish drainer and dumped the rest in. I took a slow mouthful with my eyes closed, willing the alcohol to soothe my jangled nerves, wishing I didn't have to get through another "encounter" in the form of the person standing there appraising me so aloofly.

"How's the jaw?"

"I'll never box again."

"I hope you're okay."

"Is that an apology?"

"Not yet. I have a question or two first."

"I imagine you do."

"You're up to something, Charles. That stunt with giving them the book . . . There was more to it than just surrender. Tell me."

"Not just yet, I'm afraid."

"But there is more, yes?"

"Yes."

"Does it have to do with that first story we read together . . . here . . . about the priests and giving them what they want?"

"In a manner of speaking, yes, but then nothing has gone as expected. Our first plan to make them come to us in the forest was a bust."

"Entirely?"

"I don't know quite how to answer that. We are not who we were just a few weeks ago. Maybe we weren't what we, or I, anyway, thought for a while. I, for one, am feeling very . . . uh, protective now . . . so . . ."

We stood like that in the bright glare, making what was to me a kind of unbearable eye contact. The walls that had arisen between us felt very tangible . . . impermeable. Part of me wished she would just go.

She seemed to be reading much the same script, though I may have been projecting. Who knows what's really going on in the stew of emotions and psychologies of the people we confront? Guesses.

She suddenly straightened, put down the empty glass, and stepped up close. Eyes still on mine, she leaned in and kissed me, at first softly, but then quite forcefully.

I'm not sure if in my surprise I offered any participation.

She pulled back and said, "That was an apology."

And then we were kissing with surprising fierceness. And like in a film, we left a trail of clothes from the kitchen to the bedroom where we entertained a sort of stress-releasing routine of sex, the details of which I will leave undescribed. It's not so much in squeamishness or, less, prudishness that I refrain from what might be a welcome change in the action, a little gratuitous sex, like comic relief. Rather, that the experience, while satisfactory in the mechanics of sex, was both too much and too little in other ways. It almost would have been better had we been strangers just reveling in the physical, focused solely on bodies and our own pleasures. But we knew each other better than that. We had experienced that slow increase of budding romance that is the path to love and which would include a wholly different kind of sex: what's called making love. But because of our wariness—those walls separating us—it was seemingly too late and too early for either of those sexual experiences. Too much and not enough.

So I felt regret when I woke in the morning, and making one of those guesses, I expect she felt similarly because she was gone, leaving not so much as a warm place in the bed next to me.

It's far from ideal to have to ask oneself after such an experience, "What was that about?" To wonder if the other one was in it for some ulterior motive. But there it was; I wondered if, since I had become an independent actor, she was trying to get close enough to regain some sort of control vis-à-vis the whole book/geek-thug crusade she had been on for years now. Not to mention my own motivations, my own enthusiastic contribution. What was that about? Considering all the events of the preceding day, I had the feeling that I had come down with a case of the emotional flu. I wanted to crawl back into bed and pull the covers over my head for a few days, but the bed was . . . well . . . So I settled on the couch with a pot of coffee and a head full of tangled thoughts.

-

I was sorting through some of the strange messages we get these days from strangers, the come-on job offer or sales pitch. One caught my eye. Some app developer wanted assistance from the English Department on, from what I understood through the hyperbole (yes, they needed the help), a little program in which a person (surely mostly guys would use this) could send a kind of semipersonal, semigeneric message to old flames in hopes of setting up some sort of tryst. It was laid out with these little boxes corresponding to different segments of such a message: One was the salutation, which allowed the user to choose the pet name most closely representing the one he or she used in the former relationship. Then there was some boilerplate nostalgic text with a few blanks to insert appropriate place names, then a spot for references to special sexual activities the couple had shared—again taken from a handy menu—followed finally with a prewritten line or two tastefully (?) inferring a desire to "hook up" in the future. The app would then do a digital search for the recipient of the charming proposition—solving the thorny problem of maiden name changes—and deliver it post haste. An added bonus was that the user could save drafts and, having made appropriate personalized changes suited to a variety of ex-partners, could send out a whole swarm of these postmodern Valentine cards.

Initially horrified by what had become of society, I then thought of those who might be on my own list, and then winced at the memories of the problems that brought about the dissolution of those relationships—many of my own creation. Then I thought to write a response to the misguided souls whose venture this was, illuminating their errors. Finally, reflecting on the futility of altering the viewpoint of any true believer—be it in their app, their politics, or their religion—I closed the missive and moved on to more firm deletion of other unwanted messages.

After a spate of satisfying erasures, I hesitated on another titled "Yo Prof." I opened it and saw very quickly that it was obviously a speech-to-text message. I couldn't help it. In my field, we are trained to make quick determinations of relationships of form and content.

It read, "Hey so how 'bout coming back over to the office again I have some more interp questions for ya. Just you and me no theatrics or fistfights. You'll like it your kind of philosophical lit BS having to do with a story. Say tomorrow at 10. I know you're not busy. Maurice."

In days of old, the paragraph I have reproduced would be littered with the editorial [*sic*].

Well, it was true, I hadn't much to do, though I had rather hoped for a bit of a respite from *l'affaire du livre*, as I had begun to think of it.

So it was that at the appointed hour, I was ushered by a nerdy assistant who plainly expected me into Maurice's office, which was on the other side of the building from Ray's. It was pretty tastefully decorated. I guess I had thought it would feature portraits of Der Führer or some such model conqueror, though I was reminded that Hitler had been a great lover and thief of art. Maurice did not rise to welcome me, only distractedly waved at a chair. I was somewhat surprised to see what looked like the book open before him.

"How did you pry that out of Ray's clutches?"

He smiled thinly. "Oh he's busy with the grid project. Really, that's more his speed, details, operations."

"And you're the big-picture guy?"

His eyes tightened a little as he filtered my words for sarcasm but found none, it being competently veiled, then he nodded. "Okay, you could put it that way . . . Anyway"—he tapped the book—"that's what I want to ask you about."

"I thought I had made it clear that the one reading the story was the one who was best suited to figuring out its meaning."

"Ever the professor. Don't you ever get sick of trying to educate the rabble?"

"Yes, as a matter of fact, I do."

"Well, I have learned my little lesson, thank you. I just want some background . . . some context, if you will."

"If, indeed. Why not just do a digital search?"

"I could have, but thought you might arrange the info in some . . . uh . . . insightful way. Besides, it was fun to yank your chain and get you to drag across town."

"A very cheap thrill, Maurice."

"Ah, well, we get our little pleasures where we can. I don't have the sexy Celeste to cruise with up in Oregon." He watched the shot go home and, satisfied, said, "Now, this story. You'll see that I've not closed the book. Another lesson learned, eh? I know! How about you read the story to me. It's quite short, and I'm sure you have a very . . . what's the word? A very . . . something . . . voice."

"Mellifluous? Soporific?"

"Whatever, here."

He spun the book over to my side of the desk. I picked it up and felt the comforting leather between my outspread hands.

He said quickly, "Oh and before you give in to the impulse to snap it shut, you should know that I took the precaution of scanning it just in case later reference was needed."

I smiled. I had felt that impulse twitching in my fingers. I looked at the page and read.

These Riches

The old man sipped his twenty-five-year-old scotch and looked around the magnificent room in which he sat wrapped in the deep Carrera-leather chair. He could see the gilded frames around the famous paintings he owned, the custom-designed furniture, the French windows through which, past the long green fields, floated his yacht.

He turned to his son, who had also been admiring the wealth he was heir to. The old man said, "It's not enough, son. These riches."

Surprised, the son, who was himself a grown man, replied, "What can you mean, Father? Don't we have the best of everything?

Aren't we the envy of all? Cannot we do anything we wish? Purchase things, industries? Bend our government to our will?"

"You are exactly right, son. And it is, as I said, not enough."

"What more is there, Father?" Attempting a joke, he added, "Unless you wish to rule the world."

The old man smiled and nodded and then said, "You always were a bright boy. That, of course, is it precisely."

"Are you serious? Don't we have all the influence we want? Can't we grease the political machinery whenever we want to achieve our latest goals, increase our profits, avoid taxation?"

"Yes, that is what we do. We and those like us. We do control everything for our own ends, don't you see? We are the innovators, the providers of employment, the engines of the economy, and we are rewarded highly for the service ... or so we tell ourselves. But in honesty, our wealth is extreme, and like wealthy elites from time immemorial, we achieve it through a certain amount of exploitation."

"What are you saying, Father? You sound like a liberal revolutionary who wants to redistribute wealth to the masses."

"Ah, I suppose I do, son, I suppose I do."

After a contemplative pause, the old man continued, "I am old, my boy. Ho, don't smile when I state the obvious, you rascal. I am saying that old men like me begin to see themselves as part of a larger tapestry, the great sweep of history, a piece of the development—or decline of our age. And when one does that, it becomes apparent that achieving enormous personal wealth is not so grand a legacy. No, no, don't protest. Yes, I know, this wealth has done much for our family. It will last generations. It has, indeed, provided employment for thousands and helped in that way and others to support the economy of the nation. But the equation of the wealth and the power and influence that comes with it, the precarious livings of the working classes, the dependence on us by the political classes . . . What does it add up to in that larger context of civilization?"

"Surely, Father, ours is the greatest civilization ever. Our scientific and medical advances, the freedoms all enjoy—"

The old man raised a hand. "You have learned your catechism well, son. But no, I am talking of bigger things. Our way of life is not old . . . barely a teenager compared to other civilizations of the past. And this system you have learned to defend is a house of cards. You know that. You have seen how vulnerable our financial system is, how susceptible to our machinations and, to be honest, our greed. And when it collapses, as you know it does from time to time, our class is at fault, but it is not our class that suffers. And, when you study history, you see that this is the pattern that does, indeed, lead to revolution."

"Father, this is well-known, but what would you do? Abandon the wealth, give it away? Abdicate the political power in favor of less enlightened men? And what of these noble lower orders?

Do you think they would welcome that in the long run? No, it would lead to more abuse and ruin in the long run."

The old man looked out the window for a long time, and the son felt relief, thinking he had talked the old man back from the brink. How many tycoons of the past, struck by remorse about their ruthless youths, became in the end philanthropists, endowing schools and museums for the betterment of those lower orders they had exploited?

But the old man continued, speaking quietly, "Abdication, yes, in one way, but in another, what? Noble usurpation? Perhaps."

He turned again to his son, rose from his chair, and for a moment, appeared to be the captain of industry of old.

In a firmer voice, he declared, "I am suggesting that we look to the long-term stability of our civilization, the very, very long term. We do, indeed, need a new way, a revolution, a new system. And we are the men who can do it, we and others of our class."

Again, he raised his hand to fend off the protestations even then forming on his son's lips. "I know what you are going to say, but listen. Our system is, as I said, a house of cards. The people think it is a democracy, but that is a cruel joke. They haven't the education to understand the nuances of policy, of finance. They want to be happy, have good products, believe in simple verities that can be stated in a few sentences. They don't trust the politicians with good reason. The politicians look to us for guidance. Even most of them don't understand the complexities of governing; their beliefs are expedient affectations to keep them in office.

"We, frankly, do have the education, the practical knowledge of international economies and all the rest. I know it is not politic to say these things, but everyone knows they are true. We, our class of owners of business and industry and all the rest, are those who really make the decisions, who really hold the power, who tell the people what to believe and the politicians what to do. We are oligarchs . . . not a new state of affairs in world history . . . a modern nobility class. The problem is that, like oligarchs of old, we are tainted by our own desires, ambitions, wealth, sense of superiority, insularity, and power. Thus, like oligarchies of the past, we are doomed in time to fail. And what comes after such failures? Revolutions, military coups, dictatorships, kingdoms. If we are to survive, we must truly rule, not simply pull the levers behind the curtain."

The son interjected, "Why would we want to get our hands dirty and—"

"Why? Have I not just made that clear? Survival of our civilization . . . for remember that word means much more than economy. It is the culture, the art, the science, political and international stability and longevity."

"All right, Father . . . But how? Are you suggesting a return to true democracy? The politicians, the people themselves are long-trained to be skeptical of education, so how could that work? As you say, the politicians are similarly trained to be dependent on us. Are we not, then, the best hope we have—okay, perhaps flawed, but equipped better than the others to lead?"

"You are exactly correct, son. Precisely. Only one of those groups must be improved in order to save the whole system. The simplest of them to change. Us. If we have the capabilities to direct a country—and we agree that we alone do but that our self-interests prevent our doing so in a manner that is sustaining long term for the country—we need only insulate ourselves from the temptations of our wealth. We must step out from behind the curtain and become the true, enlightened, incorruptible rulers of the country. We must rearrange society only very little. The rulers need to be put in a position of trust, which means we must disassociate ourselves from the trappings of wealth. Now, now, don't worry; I'm not advocating a vow of poverty. The rulers must be comfortable to be incorruptible. They must be highly educated, knowledgeable in all things, and wise in all things; they must understand the guiding role they have—their responsibility to the other classes and the perpetuation of peace and prosperity."

The son cried out, "Father, Father, you're talking fantasy. It's a utopia!"

"Not one that has ever been tried in the real world, son. No one has ever really done it. Oh, a few idealistic cults from century to century. But surely you can see that what I say is true, and that we are not so very far away from being able to make it happen... that it is the answer."

"Father . . . uh . . . what if I were to concede that it is as you say? What steps would need to be taken? How would one effect such a revolution without the chaos that always attends revolutions? How would you determine or develop this class of educated rulers? How would you gain the acceptance, the trust, of the people? How would you get them to give up their ideal of democracy? And the politicians . . . How could they be brought into the process?"

The old man was looking quietly at his son, a tired smile flickering along the edges of his mouth. He took a deep breath and said in a whisper that carried the pride of a father in a son, "Yes, my dear boy, those are exactly the questions you will need to ask."

It was his last breath.

I stopped reading and looked up at Maurice. I said, "Well, aren't you something to be getting stories like that . . . and that other one?"

He looked irritated and said crisply, "Look, I get it. We are beginning a new period of digital interconnectedness. Ray and I have developed a fair amount of power and influence . . . and money, yeah."

"Yeah."

"And we do view it as a cultural change and all that. But what's all this stuff about oligarchies and the elite giving up their wealth and running the government and all?"

"Plato."

"Plato?"

"I think so, yes. It sounds like his proposal for a perfect society . . . in *The Republic*."

"I'm in for another lecture, aren't I?"

“If you’d had a decent liberal arts education, you’d already know this stuff.”

“All right, all right, Professor. Let’s not make me angry again, okay?”

I nodded indulgently. “Okay. So, that one name is really all you need to do a search, but I’ll give you a little preview. Plato suggested creating a society that was ruled by a class of philosopher kings who were highly educated and trained. They were well-kept financially but insulated from all commerce . . . except in terms of government policy. They made the rules, the laws. Another class, the guardians, basically enforced the laws, managed the infrastructure of government, taxation, and the like. They, too, were well-educated but not to the level of the rulers. The rest were the people—the workers. You’ve probably heard the term, *hoi polloi*. The common people, the working class. They were also educated fairly well because they needed to understand and trust those in power and to make their various contributions to society. If you know more recent history, it is a bit like the communist system that failed so miserably. That was because the elite came from military backgrounds and felt they had to control people and outcomes—and thinking—by force. But Plato has a much more benign arrangement. Anyway, that’s the elementary bare bones of it. You can read the details.”

“And it’s never been done?”

“Well, it’s a utopia, an ideal. And all revolutions follow some ideal . . . some of which are utopian. Look no further than the American Revolution. As idealistic as they come. They tried to make it real and did a pretty amazing job . . . though the outsized power of the wealthy has been a problem from the beginning . . . and continues to be. Not to mention the problems the old guy talked about in the story.”

Maurice nodded thoughtfully.

I rose quietly and left, worrying about how a guy like Maurice would react to such a story.

Looking back at the closed door, I noticed it was blank. Curious, I approached the nerdy receptionist. She looked up from her work through the long dark fringe of her bangs and black-rimmed glasses. Her thin smile held the question.

I returned the one and asked the other. "This will seem a strange question . . . I mean, having just spent nearly two hours with him—What's his real name?"

"You don't know his name?"

"Well, people—including him—have been using this nickname, so I just never heard his given name."

"Oh, that's odd. He always uses his full name: Michael Reece. Actually, Michael O. Reece."

"Ah, clever."

"What's clever?"

"Sorry, the nickname was given by a friend. Maurice . . . M. O. Reece."

She gave a little gasp and giggled. "Moreece. That is funny. Somehow, I can't imagine us calling him that . . . Well, maybe Ray might, 'cause he's always putting him down. Oops, I shouldn't have said that. Was that disloyal? Gawd, I sometimes speak before thinking. Gotta put on the tongue brake quicker." She shook her head quickly, making her bangs flare out in a cartoony cloud and her ponytail flop.

On impulse, I asked, "Say, when do you go to lunch? Could I buy you a sandwich or something?"

She looked a little surprised and asked playfully, "Are you flirting with me, Mister . . . uh . . ." She looked at her appointment screen. "Oh . . . Professor . . ."

"Call me Charles. I'm not making a pass, just curious about the company and your boss and . . ."

"Oh, too bad. Haven't had a nice 'pass' from a distinguished professor for ages. I can leave in about five minutes. Meet you downstairs?"

I laughed. "Five minutes it is. Oh, you're . . ."

"Alice . . . PA to Maurice."

Both smiling now, we nodded, and I turned to the elevator.

-

Over a vegan dish that I couldn't quite identify, having deferred to her, we bantered trivialities. I'm certain we were both more or less circling, waiting for the real reason we were sharing lunch to arise. I wasn't certain myself; it had been a spur-of-the-moment impulse, but now I didn't know where to begin. I said as much.

She, on the other hand, seemed ready to quiz me. "Okay, so I appreciate the lunch . . ."

"But," I suggested.

"Not but . . . and . . . I am just so curious to find someone like you . . ."

I smiled. "Someone like me? Am I so easily classified?"

"Well . . . of course you are. University professor—in the English Department of all things, old enough . . . um . . . not in a bad way . . . to value old-school, as they say, education and all that. And here you are having long, unscheduled meetings with a high-tech, ambitious guy like M. O. Reece of ApolloNet. No way you two would see eye to eye on . . . well . . . anything. So my question . . . Charles . . . is, bluntly put, what the hell are you meeting him about and why the hell have you taken me out to lunch?"

I laughed. "Oh ho, is this the real Alice? First, that was two questions, and second, right when I was considering making that pass, you've gone and scared me by calling me old and questioning my motives. You are a loyal employee after all."

I could see she was trying to figure out if I was still being as playful as my tone suggested. She ate some food, which I thought a rather good ploy to get me to continue, her mouth being too busy to reply. I would have to remember that trick. Her eyes never left my face. Nor mine hers. It was an intelligent face with perceptive eyes behind the glasses and bangs, the kind of face that gets prettier as one gets to know it. But I sensed in her several layers, as if the nerdy glasses and bangs gave way to the keen eyes and recessive prettiness, below which was a canny mind.

"How long have you worked for Reece?"

"Now you're asking the questions?"

"All right. You're correct that Reece and I are not, um, natural colleagues. In fact, it would not be wrong to say that I dislike the man vigorously."

"Vigorously?"

"A lot, loads, totally . . . whatever the current idiom may be."

"I like vigorously. It suggests action, like you're putting your weight behind it. That's some good dislike you got there, Charles."

"Yes, well, I have some pretty substantial reasons."

"All the more reason to ask you why you're meeting with him. If it were a dispute, there would be lawyers in the room for sure."

"I feel as if you are getting the better of this exchange, Alice. Bravo. Shall you report—loyally—back to your employer for bonus points of some sort?"

A slow smile spread across her face, and she said, "No, he won't know . . . because in my short time working for him, I have developed several doubts myself." She let that sink in and added, "How about that, Charles? I think we're now about even. But you're right about one thing."

"What's that?"

"I do have to get back. Do you have a pen?"

I produced mine.

"A fountain pen! I love it. The classification is a lovely one, even if a bit old-fashioned."

She wrote on the back of my receipt, handed pen and paper to me, and rose. Her hand remained extended, and it took me a second to realize that she was wanting to shake mine. I half-rose and took her hand.

She dipped her head slightly and said, "Thank you for lunch. I am glad to have met you and hope we can get together again. Bye."

And just like that, she was out the door. I looked at the paper, which had her number on it. I sat back down, staring at her plate until a busboy came and took it out from under my gaze. Still thoughtful, curious, intrigued, and wary, I left.

FOURTEEN

I woke fully at 4:00 a.m. and lay for a while listening to the small sounds of the night: the refrigerator in the kitchen, the odd creaks and groans of an old building sitting atop the San Andreas fault, a distant siren. I rose and went to the window to watch the perpetual dawn of the sleeping city. Silent lights burned in static patterns across the hills and streets without really illuminating their surroundings but contributing their scant lumens to the yellow glow in the sky. There were people awake and moving, lonely, dark souls whose task it was to begin their workdays before even the sun knew the day was come. And I suppose, people like myself aplenty were gazing sleeplessly out windows at what little there was to see, seeing even less, as some stubborn thought wore a path in their brains.

I went to my computer and entered my virtual library once more. It was strange to think of all that had happened since I last acted the sleuth. The system was still configured to show intruders' glowing footprints. The inept students had retreated to their vacation revels or jobs. Celeste's unique trail, too, had grown cold. But look! There were fresh tracks glowing brightly. A thrill of outrage—or fear, perhaps—raced icily through my limbs. I picked up the trail like a bloodhound.

These footsteps seemed purposeful but uncertain . . . or omnivorous in a desire to digest as varied a meal of my digital life as possible. This was no student, no, nor a single-minded zealot like Celeste. These steps were guided by a brain that seemed to be trying to build an organizing principle through which my life's facts could be sieved.

They passed slowly, it seemed, along the row of my youth, and then lingered for quite some time exploring my academic life. I was surprised and alarmed when the trail unerringly turned toward my own recent searches as if following my own footsteps. That was a fresh jolt. If I could make my system show others' footsteps, could the reverse be true as well? It now seemed obvious to me that it could, but the realization brought with it a new sense of violation.

These thoughts had made me inattentive, and so it was yet more disconcerting when I saw I had come to the end of the trail. I stopped and looked at the glowing prints . . . two feet side-by-side facing a shelf. So . . . was this intruder even now reading what I had stored there? What was it? I looked, it felt, over this person's shoulder. Celeste's thesis! I reeled back mentally, which must have made something happen in my VR equipment because the footprints quickly turned around. It was as if we were now standing toe-to-toe, holding our breaths. What a strange intimacy this was: two invisible souls caught in surprise . . . revealed yet unseen.

The glowing prints faded and went dark. There remained no residual trace, just uniform darkness. This intruder was better at it than Celeste, and I felt afraid.

My virtual library has in it a large bay window with a comfortable chair looking out over . . . well, I could change the scene at will. Now it displayed a vast, empty plain, a gently rolling sea of varied greens devoid of other landmarks or even trees. It could be a very peaceful prospect to gaze at in thought, but it now seemed a perfect representation of my ideas and options. Although a potentially fertile landscape, it now looked unpromising, "a sterile promontory," and whatever seeds I had sown appeared inert. I could think of nothing to do but sit there in that imaginary place imagining reasons for the vague dread I felt.

I began wondering about the influence of the book among my

contemporaries. I visualized them standing separately out across the green field. It was not hard to cause images of them to be projected there.

Celeste, of course, was first. I listed the stories I could remember that she had mentioned or that we had read together. The latter caused me some heartache. How quickly that sense of kindred spirits fighting for the good of literature and the budding romance—and the flaring of passion—had evaporated. Or had it completely? Was any of it redeemable? Would I want that? Her zealotry was so monomaniacal. What if she were simply given the book? Was that the anodyne to her sickness? Surely the power of the book, the stories, the individuality of their themes enshrouded her more than anyone in our generation . . . perhaps like her great-uncle, John, who appeared to have practically disappeared into its opium-like addiction. But for Celeste, it seemed a more powerful thing still, an icon symbolic of deep Jungian currents in individual and cultural consciousness. This, too, I realized almost wincing, was my own closest point of contact with her . . . mediated by the book. Together we were deeply impressed with the story of the ancient priests and human sacrifice. That was really a motivating story for our briefly pleasant escape to the north. But that fellowship of purpose seemed to explode, so what good was that story? Or any of the stories we shared? The enigma of Celeste was too hard for me as I tried to focus on her shifting countenance before me, and I shied away to her original partner in her book-related quest: Ray.

It was impossible to know how many stories he would have been privy to. My guess is that Celeste's secretive nature would have kept even her boyfriend somewhat in the dark in much the way she obscured the book as a fictional, theoretical construct in her thesis. Eventually, he must have caught on that there was more to it. Likely, that was the genesis of their split. He certainly was infected with the perception, the belief, even mania that there was a powerful tool to be seized and used for one's own profit and aggrandizement. This revelation must have laid bare his greed to the idealistic Celeste. I looked at his image before me and noted his eyes shifting, evaluating. Perhaps she saw the same calculation in an unguarded moment as she waxed enthusiastically about the book's properties or shared a story in which he realized its potential in ambitious hands. Specifically, though, I only knew for sure that he knew the odd story about the castellan and his boat and the stolen goblet. While not a story likely to be generated in his presence, it was true that there were those of us also in the office with more literary predilections. He did react pretty strongly to my interpretation of the story, and he and Maurice picked up on the process enthusiastically. So that story must still be percolating in his head. I doubted, somehow, though, that Maurice had shared the latest one about the old man and his son—the Plato's *Republic* story.

Maurice (as I still thought of him), then, had moved on to this new story. I don't think he much cared for being forced to think in such historical and philosophical pathways. No, he was a product of his age, the age of now, that reflects little or not at all on where we have been and how we got here. Such people think of what is here in the moment and only far enough into the future to imagine new technologies, not so much for their utility but for their monetization and popularity. He and Ray had been further bitten by the bug of ambition for influence and power, but this was really just an extension of the ethos of which they were already a part. However, Maurice seemed to me to be not yet, but on the cusp, of being torn by this new set of ideas. He was seeing for the first time that there might be grander ideas at play in the world, higher stakes than those his simple avarice had heretofore revealed. Where would these thoughts lead him? I had no illusions about his character, though. I had seen his streak of malevolence at close hand and had no faith that he would be washed clean by the utopian ideals of Plato. He had, though, taken pains to preserve that story. He had scanned it for future reference. Then I stopped cold.

Had he scanned it, or had his personal assistant done the task? Alice now appeared next to the others on my green field. Had she read the story? Did that explain her caginess over lunch? What might she have made of it . . . and her boss's own caginess?

Had he sent her to have lunch with me to make sure I was well caged? But I had invited her. She had certainly played it smoothly. Her probing curiosity appeared more ominous now. Was it she who had searched my files, who I had just encountered, our digital feet only inches apart? It began to feel that it could be no one else. But why the detailed search of my past? And why would she end up reading Celeste's thesis? That was doing her job a bit overzealously. Surely Maurice wouldn't direct her to dig so deeply. And, I kept circling back to it, those questions at lunch . . . between them and her poking through my library—no, not poking through; she was systematically exploring. Again, why? Not tasked by Maurice nor, I think, by Ray. What then? Her own curiosity? No, surely not. Now the question became: Who is this woman Alice? And what's she up to?

I looked on the ApolloNet website, slid past the usual glossy hyperbole, and under employees found her name, photo, and a brief bio. It seemed she had not been there long but sounded very well qualified for the position. I began searching elsewhere and discovered a more detailed curriculum vitae. It, too, was impressive . . . a seemingly precise blend of technology training and organizational experience. I was impressed at how well suited she seemed to be for working as Maurice's personal assistant. But there was nothing that suggested her motives for ransacking my history.

I decided to dig more deeply, if possible. I looked up her schools, graduation dates, and departments, then looked for her own thesis. And it was there that I found the first real clue. Although listed in her CV, there was no thesis. In fact, her name was not on the list of graduates. Perhaps she had been married and now, or then, used a different last name. I rooted along that trail for a while and still found no satisfactory explanation. That thesis should be listed by title, which I had. It did not seem to exist. It had seemed so perfect for someone applying to ApolloNet. The CV, too, had seemed a little too perfect, and now it looked as if it might be a fabrication. If so, to what end? To get a high-paying job? That was common enough, the padding or fabrication of a résumé to land a higher-level position than one deserved. But somehow that didn't feel quite right. Alice did seem learned, and while she may have prevaricated and dissembled in our conversation, she did not seem dishonest.

I realized that I had just stepped out on the thin ice of believing what I hoped to be true . . . a common enough fault in my profession.

What motive would she have, then? Dishonesty seemed at the core of her employment. But then my own motives were a little tangled as well. Not that that should give her a pass. So was she, say, working for a rival company? It was undeniable that ApolloNet had pretty much shouldered its way into the national economic scene with its mastery of the technical means of communication and control, having leaped from the level of internet connections to the means of operating the entire national electrical grid, among other activities. The old guard must feel very threatened indeed to have such lucrative and influential power wrested from their hands—especially, for most people, the takeover having come through such an esoteric method. It was like someone's body being taken over via the unseen and mysterious autonomic nervous system. And ApolloNet could probably manipulate access and service in a variety of ways to influence a variety of outcomes favorable to themselves. Heady power. Ray and Maurice must be spinning with it. Yes, she could very easily be a spy from such big business eager to recoup losses and power from what they must consider a usurpation of their traditional, now entitled, position. And this would, of course, be tied to their long-standing lobbying activities in government.

This line of analysis was getting rather too realpolitik for an English professor, and I felt myself shying from the whole thing.

Of course, though, I couldn't turn off the loop in my brain. I did, however, turn off the VR rendering of my green field with the lifelike chess pieces of my life that had been the backdrop of my other investigations. I was surprised to find that not only was it full day but the morning was well advanced. The fading image of the field in my brain allowed but one more thought to be gleaned . . . coffee.

-

As the coffee began buzzing around the edges of my exhaustion, the image surfaced of Stoppard's Rosencrantz, dizzied by the swirl of characters and events beyond his ken, looking wild-eyed toward the stage wings, not knowing who would spin him and Guildenstern in new directions, shouting, "Neeeext."

Then Hamlet was declaiming in my head about "some craven scruple of thinking too precisely on the event" and "a thought which, quartered, hath but one part wisdom and ever three parts coward."

"Bloody hell," I replied, "I'll just go confront one more woman about another little spying escapade in my system!"

In short order, I was lurching with unkempt resolution out the elevator doors toward Alice's desk. She was leaning forward, speaking with quiet intensity to a woman, who also leaned in. The conspiratorial impression was just settling into my dull-witted head when the second woman turned at the sound of my approach. Celeste.

All three of us stood in a display of surprise and wariness. Both women straightened and said simultaneously, "Charles." They looked briefly at each other as if in response to my first name being used by them both.

This gave me a tiny moment to catch my balance and scrape rapid fingers through my hair, as well as try to decide if I should mention my errand in the presence of the two trespassers into my library. Before I could decide, loud voices erupted from behind Maurice's office door, which then was flung open by none other than an enraged Ray who was shouting back at Maurice that buying politicians was how it worked, and besides, they had him in the bag from the grid threat anyway.

Whirling around, he saw our frozen tableau. He spun back to Maurice, shouting, "Are these people here about that damn book again? I told you we don't need it anymore! It's just making you act crazy! Wake up, you idiot; we're almost there!"

One more spin, a hateful glare, and he was gone.

"Oh my God, that's . . ." Alice was staring at the receding Ray. She took a decisive step toward the elevator, checked herself, and turned back.

But Celeste was on the move. She strode into the office where Maurice stood red-faced, furious. Celeste swooped over the desk like an osprey and snatched the book, which still lay open. "I'll take that." She turned and marched past me, adding, "If you have no objection, Professor."

With a sharp ding from the elevator bell that reminded me for a painful second of her father's shop, she, too, departed.

A slamming door behind me caused me to spin once again to see the vibrating door of Maurice's office. The noise, the constant spinning back and forth, and my exhaustion made me stagger slightly from dizziness. Then Alice was right there, steadying me by the shoulders.

"Charles, are you all right?"

"Yes, I just got a little dizzy for a second. Thank you."

I was looking into her concerned eyes and felt comforted, as if really seeing her for the first time. I remembered standing this close to her in virtual reality in my library, toe-to-toe. That, too, was intensely intimate, but of a wholly different nature. I think she was thinking the same thing.

What I said, though, was, "Celeste . . ."

Her hands slid off my shoulders, but her guard did not come back up. "Yes?"

"You read her thesis."

With eyes still on mine, no dissimulation, she said, "Yes. Yes, I read . . . most of it. That's the book, right?"

"It is."

"Charles, there is something very important I must do now. We need to talk further, but later."

Then she, too, rushed off to the elevator. Another ding, some whirring, then silence.

"Dramatis personae exeunt," I mused. So I followed off stage right and down to the street, which was shrouded in dense, wet fog. It suited me perfectly, and before long, I had made it to my bed, where I fell instantly into a deep, foggy sleep.

FIFTEEN

California is often thought of preceded by the adjective *sunny*. It's often a sunny place: warm beaches, hot deserts, sun-dappled meadows. But residents of the state are very familiar with the negation of sunshine: fog. From the tule fog that blankets vast San Joaquin Valley, terrifying motorists and vital to agriculture, to the famous marine layer, the June gloom, that rolls onto nearly eight hundred miles of coastline. Fog can linger for days, and it can appear almost in an instant, riding a sudden sea breeze caused by the heating of the land, which creates convection of the air rising up and pulling air off the ocean. And later in the day, it can "burn off" nearly as quickly. It is thus almost magically transitory and strangely lingering; it is beautiful, quiet, and threateningly impenetrable. It is cooling on a hot day; it is damp and chilling on a cool one.

Growing up along the coast, I have many memories of fog: Walking to elementary school holding hands with my big brother who I literally could not see, surprised that our parents sent us out in it. It seemed amazing that we could find our way to school at all, and I clung tightly to the invisible hand that towed me blindly down the hill, turning into the dirt alleyway and to the complicated intersection of streets and railroad tracks and the dubious assistance of the stern old crossing guard in her military uniform. And in boats on a perfectly tranquil blue sea that mirrored the sky, only to watch a towering tidal wave of gray cloud swoop over the horizon and engulf our boat, leaving us wondering just how far we were from shipping lanes. Fog is, among so many things, a great changer of moods. It is a trigger to whatever introvert tendencies one may have. Introspection comes naturally in fog.

I had slept only little that late morning after the excitement at ApolloNet. And then I went out to wander in the fog. It was probably a six on a density scale of ten, thick but navigable. Remembering those little anecdotes from my youth reminded me of what Mr. Lathke had said about us being, one and all, storytellers. I missed the wise old dilettante, our easy intellectual, multifaceted conversations. Finding, with some small surprise, that I had wandered into the general neighborhood of his atelier, I continued, thinking to ask of my friend (I dared call him this in spite of the imbroglio he had drawn me into).

I knocked with some apprehension on the door, marked now by an Out of Business sign. The obvious realization had only just then arisen in my brain that it would be Celeste, if anyone, who answered the door.

Indeed, it was her wary face that appeared in the narrow aperture.

"Oh, hi," I stuttered. Was I really about to say, "I was just in the neighborhood?"

She waited.

I tried again. "Celeste, I'm not here about the book. Honest."

"Cross your heart?"

"And hope to die."

"That hope will surely come to pass."

"Uh, right . . . for all of us, of course. But, no, I was thinking about your father and realized that I missed the codger, and . . . out wandering in the fog . . . and . . ."

"You'd better come in, then."

She led the way into the shop, and I closed the door, saying, "I should get you a bell."

She stopped and turned. "Pardon?"

"A bell, a Dickensian bell. I always think I hear one when I walk through that door. It's like walking into the Old Curiosity Shop."

She lifted her chin slightly, showed a hint of a smile, and continued into the shop.

Looking around, I was startled that it seemed little changed. Instruments still hung on the wall, though less densely, and the tools on the workbench looked as if they had only just been put down.

"I thought he had disposed of all the instruments."

"He has found various homes for quite a few. It's just that he had so many. He has been enjoying placing each with some appropriate new owner: a collector here, a museum there, some sold for very substantial sums, others given away for various sentimental reasons, like those he gave us."

This gave us both pause, remembering our music-making in this evocative space.

"That's where he is now, delivering a special cello. As you might imagine, after a lifetime in the business, he has contacts across the country, indeed, worldwide. There is a young Italian man living in Florida who is carrying on the old techniques of cello making, so Dad is surprising him with a visit and a gift. He is having so much fun."

"The conversations he must be having."

We fell silent, smiling, imagining spry Mr. Lathke talking earnestly and broadly with each of these people: the craftsmen, the academics . . . the dilettantes.

"Oh, to be a fly on the wall," I said.

"Yes. Coffee?"

I nodded and followed her back to the little kitchenette I remembered from that first visit.

"So will he come back? Will he, or you, keep the rest of the . . . uh, family"—I gestured to the walls—"together?"

"He probably won't come back here. He, incidentally, has a place in a very nice retirement village in Florida not far from that cello guy, and has given me the shop and all it holds. Besides, he was pretty frightened by, what do you call them? The geek thugs. So it's just me and the dusty old instruments. And, I guess I should say it, the book."

"Which, I reassert is not the reason for my visit."

"Okay, then. Here's your coffee, I believe the way you like it."

"Thank you. Yes, perfect."

Turning back to the heart of the shop, she said, "Let's sit."

We walked over to several old, comfortable chairs and sat in silence, nursing the French roast and letting our eyes wander along the rows of instruments. There remained quite a variety, and there were some I still could not identify.

After a goodly while, I said, "I do love my little rajão . . . and its sweet story. It is so . . . something . . . don't laugh if words fail the English professor. As your father and I spoke of, music is one of those things, or experiences, that transcend our ability to communicate about, or analyze. So the rajão and its history, the Madeira Islands, the little girl on the ship to Hawaii, and especially its sweet little voice . . ."

"Preaching to the choir, Charles. But I am very glad you feel that way. The fiddle brings with it a panoply of feelings and stories too . . . many connected to my childhood."

After more silence and pondering of these thoughts, I said, "I imagine each of these instruments has a story it could tell. But I better go. Please give my regards to Mr. Lathke when you speak to him. Thank you."

I made to rise, but Celeste held up a hand, saying, "Charles, wait a few moments. There is something I want to share with you."

She rose, went to the workbench, and brought back the book. My heart stopped, but I held my peace, hoping that we weren't about to renew our conflict after such a pleasant tête-à-tête. I noticed the book was already open, as if she didn't want to lose the story she had found there.

Sensing my concern, she said, "I just want to read you a story I found earlier . . . what you just said . . ."

She turned to the front of the story and began.

The Immortal Song
by Arial McInnes

He was an impoverished young harpist, an apprentice. His master performed for the nobles, but the apprentice did not, for he had one gift, that of music, but the other gift he had not, words. In that day, words and music were married in song and one was rarely seen out of the company of the other. Yet the apprentice had composed a sublime melody, one that in another era might be thought to transcend words, but in his was but a spinster. Alone and lonely, he wandered among dusty shelves of forgotten books . . . old bachelors. One came to hand, as such things often happen in such tales, resistant to explanation. Turning at random, he came across the simple lyric:

Lady . . . youth, snowy skin abloom with spring's first roses

Your treasures abound

From sky-cast eye to fruited breast and damasked limb

While the sun rides in your hair

Ere long may we not kiss

And be lost as lovers are lost

In timeless embrace?

He realized that in these words, he had found the perfect mate for his melody. He married them and practiced and practiced until he felt he could perform the piece flawlessly. He dared ask his master if he could play it for him, and the master, being kind, acquiesced. The apprentice played it as well as he could, almost perfectly. The old master was very impressed, for the young man seemed to possess talent beyond that which had hitherto been evident.

And then the master perceived that he might take the work of his apprentice and present it as his own. It was easy enough to justify, for have not apprentices contributed to works of art of their masters without credit before? Were they not lucky to have been allowed the opportunity to thus participate and learn? That was the very system. However, the conscience of the master smote his heart, and he remembered how bright and tenuous was the creative flame in his own youth, how easily blown out. No, his role was to feed the tiny spark, and so he praised the young man and announced that he would perform his piece before the court that very evening.

So it was that after the evening repast had been cleared and sated nobles sipped their wine and nibbled sweetmeats in the warm glow of candles and hearth, the master harper introduced his young protégé with effusive praise.

The apprentice approached the musicians' dais and nodded gravely to his master and then to those of great station seated and reclined nearby. It was not the nearness of the fire that caused his face to glow so brightly.

He sat, placed his small harp on his lap, and closed his eyes. He determinedly concentrated on the music and the words, trying to blot out the faces that looked at and perhaps judged him. He opened his eyes—for he had been taught that a performance must be communicated to the audience through the eyes as well as voice—and began. As he finished the musical introduction and came to the lyrics, his eyes found two other eyes that were very widely and innocently gazing at his. To these he sang. And they, on their part, encouraged him and seemed never once to stray or even blink. He became gradually aware that the eyes belonged to a face, a girl's face of nearly his years. It was a beautiful, though not flawless, face, akin somehow to his song. He sang the words to her, and somehow her eyes and very expression of being helped him, joined him, and responded to the lines:

Lady . . . youth, snowy skin abloom with spring's first roses

Your treasures abound

From sky cast eye to fruited breast and damasked limb

While the sun rides in your hair

Ere long may we not kiss

And be lost as lovers are lost

In timeless embrace?

When the song finished, the eyes of all the elders in the room shone with tears, for the song reminded them of their youths and the first stirring of love and passion. But the eyes of the apprentice and the high nobleman's daughter, for that was who she was, remained bright and dry and focused on their counterparts.

At evening's end, the apprentice walked slowly along a dimly lit gallery, replaying his triumph. He felt his hand tugged from behind. Startled, he turned and looked again into the wide eyes of the nobleman's daughter. Now it was her cheeks that glowed. She clutched his hand in both of hers and exclaimed, "I have never heard such a song nor been so moved by music." She blushed further, realizing, perhaps, that she had admitted to not merely an idealistic heart but also a nature alive to the prospect of passion.

The apprentice, never golden tongued, was further stripped of language, and under the intoxication of music, praise, and beauty, leaned forward and kissed her, to which she responded readily.

The spell lasted but seconds before some stray sound wedged the reality of their untenable situation into their minds, and they pulled rapidly apart. But it was too late. An ill-fated love flared between them, and there remained then only the means by which they would be ravaged by it.

The girl's father, in fact, was an observant man and had noticed his daughter's response to the music. And having been young once as well, could well-enough imagine the rest . . . far beyond what the two youngsters could see, in spite of the hesitation they had felt. He knew that they would be innocent enough to be unable to withstand such heady attraction, and disaster would be its fruit, and perhaps a child into the bargain.

By morning, he had arranged a journey with a small entourage into the great capital city, where they would partake of the culture and learning that throve there. His daughter would be exposed to the larger world, the expectations and opportunities of her class, and, if lucky, would make a fine match there before long, for his was a wealthy and noble lineage and she a rare beauty.

Of musicians on such a journey there would be no need, for the capital was a gathering place of the best of the best from the known world.

As the train of carriages, servants, nobles on steeds, and the lot streamed out of the courtyard, the two pairs of eyes again sought each other out, but this time they were not dry.

The nobleman's machinations worked to perfection, and the head and heart of his daughter were filled to overflowing with the sights and sounds of all the world come to the great capital: cultures, tongues, arts and letters, endless gay parties . . . and suitable suitors aplenty.

The apprentice during this time—and it was a long time indeed, nearly a year—needing to earn his bread, continued his studies with the master. Eventually, this took him, too, from the nobleman's city, but alas, never to the great capital.

Thus, the tiny spark of love was extinguished before ever it could take flame. No, that is not quite right. For the apprentice was, like many artists, inspired by lost loves, and he composed many a fine melody with a melancholy air. Never again did he, though, venture to put words to his music.

The girl became, of course, a fine lady who had married well and brought into adulthood a number of honorable offspring beyond those one or two that had died young, as is so often the case in this world. She was lucky as well that she, too, lived to a ripe age, the dangers of childbearing being as they were. And were we to question the lady of her ancient flirtation with the youthful musician, she might barely remember it.

But it was true that she did sometimes sing a pretty love song of old and enigmatic provenance, and even taught it to her children as a quaint, naive song of another age. Thus, the song was passed down through the generations and it is known to us today, although the names of the wordsmith, the musician, and the girl have long been forgotten.

It is an immortal song.

Celeste's voice seemed to echo slightly in that room full of tuned strings. I had the fancy there that every string was humming.

But, although I could see something in Celeste's face that bespoke a certain tenderness, I knew that I was on a slippery slope for several reasons. It was not time to tell her my secret, nor did I want to put at risk this thaw in our relationship. With polite thanks, I excused myself. I smiled as best I was able into her perplexed eyes.

In gray contemplation, I walked home pondering this incomplete rapprochement with Celeste. It might have been more complete if not for my withholding. And I had not forgotten her volatility. Such as it was, I was as near content as I had any reason to expect, or rather, further from turmoil, perhaps, is a better characterization.

SIXTEEN

I was tinkering in my virtual library, trying to begin preparations for the coming semester, but I kept getting distracted—an old book here, a group of near-forgotten photos there. I was beginning to think that I would just have to wait for that dreaded faculty back-to-school in-service day before I could get motivated. They worked, after a fashion. Administrators would cobble together some kind of program with an inspiring speaker, some newfangled (read: reinvented) teaching technique, a cringe-inducing team-building exercise, followed by a somnambulant department meeting. All of this, of course, served the simple purpose of a sharp slap across the cheek meant to convey the message, "Break's over! Time to wake up and actually earn your salary!" The day was so dreadful that we were all too ready to escape into our classes. It was a relief, then, to stop the pretense of preparation when a message bell rang in my headset.

The voice was that of Alice. "Hey, Charles, what's up?"

I was a little taken aback by this familiarity but gathered a few of my wits and replied, "Oh, Alice. Hey. Just wandering in my virtual library trying to get motivated for work . . . failing miserably. You?"

"Oh, really? Hang on . . ."

After a brief silence, the shelves of my virtual library shimmered, and a 3D image, an avatar, appeared before me. It looked just like her.

"Hello, Professor. May I come in?"

I snorted, activated my own avatar image so she could see me, and said with as little irony as I could, "Certainly. *Mi casa, su casa*."

"Touché, Charles, touché. But . . . what's with the getup?"

I remembered then how I had programmed my personal representation to look.

"Oh, right. A little joke really . . . English professor in his library wearing a smoking jacket and slippers, pipe smoking merrily on the desk. Of course, you can't smell the smoke. Can't stand the stuff, but as the old Hollywood directors knew, smoke is very photogenic. Anyway, welcome . . . uh, back. I won't offer a tour, I think."

Though her image did not reply, it did smile. She was standing quite close to me—VR being as convincing as it is—and I was reminded of the last time we stood virtually in this space, almost touching. She looked completely herself: hair pulled back in a no-nonsense ponytail, black blouse over black pants, and her trademark glasses. Fetching in a New York or London kind of way.

"You're good at banter, Charles. I like that, intellectual, ironic, a hint of undercurrent. So I just . . . uh, stopped by, as it were, to see if you'd like to . . . um, hang out a bit . . . uh, not here, nice as it is . . ."

Was she a little nervous? I suddenly didn't want to chase her away with my cleverness.

"Sure, that would be nice. Where? When?"

Was I a little nervous?

"Do you know that little pub, If the Shoe Fits? I think it's not far from you."

"Oh, right. I have been meaning to go there . . . when I wasn't, you know, so busy. Ha!"

"In an hour, say?"

"Oh, an hour! Well, okay, sure."

"That'll give you time to change and wash the smell of smoke out of your hair. See ya then, cheers!"

The image dissolved, and I resolved for once to refrain from analysis and to just get going.

-

If her bangs and multilayered eyes and face had been intriguing in the full light of day, they were doubled here in the woody pub booth. Attractive women do have that advantage over men who are seemingly so willing to be thrown off stride by appearances. I once chided a female friend for using her looks to sway her boss, and she replied that one can't blame a girl for using what works. It was such a pragmatic use of male sexism that I was rather disturbed by the cool calculation.

I said nothing of all this, of course, only observing that her avatar was a remarkably close facsimile, right down to the black outfit and ponytail.

She smirked and said, "My dear professor, you are not quite as up to date, technologically speaking, as one in your august profession ought to be."

"Cheeky."

We laughed, unbent a bit, ordered drinks, and sat back in relatively comfortable silence.

With our drinks half-gone and after desultory commonplaces, Alice put her elbows on the table and said, "Since we hardly know each other, it seems normal that we might ask questions. I don't want to come across as if I'm . . . um . . . interrogating you, but I am curious."

I chose to reply to a different part of her statement than I imagine she intended. "How do you want to come across?"

She smiled. "Curious."

"Okay, then, begin."

"All right. No significant other? Celeste, for instance?"

"Funny, I think she asked me much the same question. I believe I mentioned a story about a classic train platform goodbye, but the truth is like most people these days, I have had a couple of long-term relationships that never quite turned into marriage . . . longevity statistics being what they are. There was no—what's the old word? *Issue*—from the relationships. Now I am beginning to feel the notion of issue . . . offspring . . . children . . . may be the most significant part of life I am missing. How about you?"

"Are you asking if I want to have kids with you, Charles? Ask me again after my second drink."

We laughed softly and each took a sip.

"Oh, you want to know if I have had offspring in or outside of marriage! No, not even close. Nerdy career girl such as I . . ."

"Are you a career girl?"

Oh ho! A hit, a palpable hit. Her eyes flickered briefly behind the glass as she processed the import of my question. Could she know that I had tried researching her background—as she had mine—and come up with seeming smoke and mirrors?

I rescued her. "As for Celeste, we did seem to hit it off there for a while, but she is kinda . . ."

"Intense? Driven?"

"Yeah, those will do, I suppose. I did—do—really like her dad. That's how we met. He has, or did have, this little old-world instrument shop. I took my guitar there for adjustment, and we had a great, meandering conversation. So yeah, I met Celeste through him, but she's got a fair amount of baggage from her old boyfriend, Ray, and differing attitudes about academic ethics and stuff."

"Differing from him or you?"

"Both, I suppose."

"Is that to do with that weird book thing? You know Maurice had me copy it, and she took it off his desk, right?"

It was time, then, for me to move into deeper waters. "Yes, that's the book, if you want to call it that. I think of it more as a literary device, a metaphor. But you know about all that from reading her thesis in my library."

She took a sip—that stalling method I remembered from our lunch—and dove in. "Yes, about that. Listen, Charles, I owe you an apology for that. Guess you have another obsessive lady on the edge of your life."

She smiled self-deprecatingly and continued, "I was brand-new on the job of this rapidly expanding but somewhat secretive company that had just scored an amazing coup in setting up a completely new master control of the electrical grid. That's huge and has vast implications . . . satellites and stuff. My boss—bosses, really, I guess—are these brilliant, ambitious tech guys who seem a bit ruthless. You don't think they are cutting corners, you know, doing anything illegal, do you?"

That was a bit of a surprise question, as if wedged purposely in.

"Well, I don't know anything about all that, but just a few brief encounters with those guys were enough to send me happily scurrying back to academia. *Amoral* may be how I would describe them. I'd be careful if I were you. But, back to your apology."

"Oh, right. So I'm trying to find my way in all this, and in walks this English professor, who seems to have the ear of these guys, but they resent the hell out of him. And there's this story that somehow is causing conflict with the bosses. It was really confusing and unpredictable . . . and, frankly, it just made me so darned curious. So, having no significant other or offspring, I guess I let my curiosity blossom in my free time . . . and . . . um . . . started snooping. Uh, well, sorry?"

"Is that a question?"

"What? Oh, I guess I inflected that way. I guess I was asking if you forgive me."

Her eyes were steady now. She didn't seem to be dissembling. Neither did she seem to see that I still had some doubts. I felt we had come to a comfortable point of détente, equals, potential friends, and that was fine for now.

I finished my drink, then looked at her directly and sincerely and said, "Yes, Alice, I do forgive you. Perhaps we can do it again sometime."

Her cheer had returned, and she asked cheekily, "Drinks, apologies, or having offspring?"

I said, "All three!"

We laughed, and she snatched up the check.

On my way home, I realized that I was in a similar position with both Alice and Celeste: kinda close but with reservations . . . which went both ways in each case. This thought and the return of the fog made my mood sink. Entering my home, I sat in the chair next to the couch and pictured Celeste there in her cat pose. It can be difficult to live alone. All our gadgetry does not make it easier in certain ways. I imagine that the true introvert who thrives on solitude and one-on-one friendships is fine. The true extrovert, who is fueled by the group, will probably always find a way to build a crowd or a party or some sort of lively social group, so is also probably content. But what of the ambivert? The one who needs both group interaction and time alone to think or create, who gets drained by too much group energy yet bored and lonely with too much solitude.

I knew I was in this latter group. With the advent of, and gradual conversion to, the virtual university, I had lost the regular yet limited small-group environment in which I thrived . . . *throve* in the old usage to which I clung. I was much more alive, more mentally acute, quicker of thought and association in the class setting. I could see every face, who was getting it, who needed me to circle back in some fresh way, who would benefit from small-group work. I still saw the value in the occasional spirited lecture. I had profited mightily in my own schooling from listening to very intelligent people talk about things at a high level, weaving ideas together in ways I hadn't known possible, inspiring a small group of us who were thus eager to rev up our brains to some degree worthy of our professor. No tossing the teacher-centered classroom completely out the window in favor of the student-centered class . . . blind leading the blind. Of course, such simplifications are . . . just that.

At any rate, I did quite miss the eye contact, the watching for the lights to come on, the sheer performance of the professor role. It could be quite profound, intimate in a way, certainly funny at times. And then to go home to a quiet house was delicious. I suppose that group interaction, the single shared focus is much of why people go to church. Not the megachurch with its swaying songs and rock beat. I had been to many a concert and felt exactly the same transcendent beauty and sense of belonging. Yes, the spirit moves in such places, but how can one know it is not the powerful spirit of music? But the small churches had at least a more personal sense of individual personalities coming together. They used a fine word for it: *fellowship*. That word, of course, can be applied to far more situations than houses of worship; any group or club could claim it. But perhaps the ones that cause participants to come together to create, or somehow be inside, music are the richest.

In any case, sitting there in the quiet, dark, and lonely house, I could almost feel an eagerness to go to the upcoming college in-service. At least we still met in the physical building, where, completely apart from the machinations of administrators, we met up with colleagues and caught up with their lives, activities, reading, trips, ideas for the semester. Better it would be if the college would just leave us to our own devices and let us mingle, socialize, share, and eat together, rather than weigh us down with the pretense of importance. By the end of such days we were otherwise reduced to our high school algebra class selves, collectively urging the clock toward release.

I thought half-seriously that maybe Celeste and I should start a band.

SEVENTEEN

Shortly thereafter, I was indeed mingling with colleagues, trying to juggle a cheap pastry, bad coffee, and noneducational conversations with people I really only saw in person at these functions. The colleague with whom I had worked on my recent extracurricular project had just approached and begun asking me how it had turned out when his face went dark. Everything went dark. There was a brief silence and then laughter, as we all realized we had been saved by a power outage. We stood around for a bit in the dim light cast by the clerestory windows, making jokes and wondering what was going on. Then a voice rose above the murmuring, exclaiming that it was a citywide outage and the event was canceled. This announcement was greeted with cheers, and I felt a momentary sympathy for whatever motivational speaker was thus deprived of inspiring us, but the feeling quickly passed, and I made my way out of the building.

It was a typical hazy, late-summer morning, so there was little enough evidence of the power being down. I had driven my old car down, and as I proceeded toward home, I did see street signals were out and business signs were deprived of luminance and their normal annoying flashing. Traffic, of course, was a mess. Then I noticed lots and lots of people on the sidewalks, many looking back and upward into the buildings they had just exited. I realized that elevators would be without power except in those buildings that had backup generators. California earthquake codes being what they were, there were many modern structures that were thus provided for. Many smaller, older buildings, though, would take more effort to get out of. It didn't seem like this outage would really cause all that much inconvenience, just the equivalence of a snow day elsewhere.

It took quite a while to get home, but eventually I made it. Approaching my building, I saw the first real problem. The door had a hardwired electronic keypad. Several of us milled at the doorway, imagining spending the night on the street, but then someone from inside opened the door with the emergency handle, propped it open with a trash bin, and we made our way to . . . oh, right, not the elevators. We flocked to the stairway, stomping up and peeling off at various floors with muttered versions of "*Bonne chance*," "*Buena suerte*," and the like. My apartment being high up, I now paid the price for my view with burning quadriceps.

Luckily, my door still used a key lock, so I was okay getting in. I realized now that there must be thousands not so lucky standing before some fancy electronic home-security apparatus. Once in, I reflexively flicked a switch. Oh, right, no power, Einstein. I opened every drape and curtain in the place, and all seemed pretty normal, until I decided to make some coffee. "Oh, right, Einstein" became my mantra for the rest of the day. I didn't want to open the fridge, as at least now whatever food was in there, and it wasn't all that much, would stay cold longer if untouched. *Ha*, I thought, *I could starve trying to preserve my food!* I did remember that somewhere I had a few candles left over from some rather distant romantic dinner. Had Celeste and I eaten under candlelight? No, surely not. Wasn't that when she broke into my home? I remembered we had shared some pretty fair wine, though. So I inventoried what survival gear I had, essentially a few candles and matches and a goodish stock of wine, and sat down and looked at the wall, thinking, thinking, and thus mesmerized, dozed.

I woke and remembered my mobile. *Oh, right, Einstein, you got power and a link to the outside world . . . at least as long as the battery holds out. Besides,* I chided myself, *why are you thinking like it's doomsday? The power with be back on, probably in the next hour, and it's only been a few hours so far. Oh, wait, how long was I sleeping? Why in the middle of the morning?* The light in the room was now completely different. It was afternoon!

I began looking for news, but entire swaths of the internet were dark. The more I looked for a variety of sources, the farther afield the outage seemed to be affecting. In fact, it was only when I tried looking at international news sources that I came to realize that apparently, improbably, the main providers of power for the entire nation were off-line. I saw headlines like, "US Goes Dark," "Hear That Silence? USA Out Like a Light," and "America Powers Down." There was rampant speculation about terrorism, incompetent employees, a lightning strike on some main facility, and solar storms. But the one consistent thread was that the problem was confined to the continental United States and a few Canadian areas unfortunately connected to the same grid.

Engrossed in the search, I realized, finally, that I had been at it too long and I had better preserve my battery.

Wait, I thought. *ApolloNet is running the power grid, right? What was it Alice had said about implications? Satellites? No way!*

I got up and went to the door, paused, went back to the kitchen, and grabbed a candle and a bottle of wine, then popped, well, dragged down the stairs. I had no idea where Alice lived, but Celeste would be fun to spin conspiracy theories with . . . and I knew for sure that old Mr. Lathke would have had no truck with some newfangled electronic door lock.

—

I knocked on the shop door several times and waited. A window above opened, and Celeste's head appeared. She wordlessly dropped a key that spun in the sunlight. I missed the catch, and by the time I picked the key up, the window had closed. Somewhat mystified, I let myself in, content now with the silent door, which I locked behind me. The shop was eerily quiet and dim, the remaining instruments, and there were numerous, hanging mute, their many strings still in the musty air.

I made my way to the back of the shop and felt my way up the dark stairs, where I found the apartment door open. I went in quietly.

"Celeste?"

She sat on the sofa by the window with legs pulled up, looking at the floor. My stomach clenched in dread. Sitting next to her, I took her hand, and she leaned her head on my shoulder.

I whispered, "Not your dad?"

Almost imperceptibly, she nodded. I squeezed her hand, and words fled before the magnitude of death. We sat veiled in grief while memories processed in our minds.

After a long while in silence in the gradual diminution of sunlight, Celeste said, "Why don't you open that wine."

I brought a couple glasses from the kitchen and sat back down. Knowing better than to begin asking questions, I sat quietly with my shoulder just touching hers to remind her she wasn't alone.

She had sipped at her wine until the glass was nearly empty before she spoke. "The power outage killed him."

"What? It's been less than a day . . . wha . . ."

"That's not all, of course, but . . ."

I took her glass from her hand and put both glasses on the steamer trunk coffee table, enveloping her in my arms from the side, trying to stifle my questions.

Her voice was quite soft now. "A perfect train of disasters . . . He was sick there in Florida. He had COVID-19 . . ."

I stiffened, remembering the horrifying pandemic. Again, the questions rose, but, in a slow, halting cadence, she continued, "Yes, the vaccine. He never could take any of those because of his various allergies to the stuff they make them with. So flus and those kinds of things . . . he was always vulnerable. Then he got it somehow. He was in the hospital. I was on my way to the airport. They had him on a ventilator, so chances were fair. But the power went down. They had a backup generator, but when it ran out of fuel, they couldn't get more or pump—gas stations are down or somehow something . . . The electricity just went down . . . and . . . and . . . it just didn't take that long . . ."

I was stunned. She was right, a perfect train of disasters. The power outage was . . . wow. A preventable death—of one of the world's most lovely souls.

We mourned together as night fell above his magical, anachronistic instrument shop.

Later we descended into the dark atelier and wandered in careful candlelight. It seemed now to be even more of another age in that wavering and weak yellow light that illuminated only nearby objects, and those in Rembrandt hues of brown and golden woods overlaid with ever-deeper and multi-shaped shadows, punctuated with tiny metallic reflections. Celeste stopped here and there, looking not just at instruments but also tools, the workbench, clamps, jigs, and arcane materials of the luthier. These dim items stimulated free associations in her mind, and almost to herself, she gave them voice: recollections, stories, fragments of conversations that had passed in that place. Her words were like a meandering eulogy, almost a paean to the life of the artisan, her father and my friend.

Among the artifacts, she came across an old beetle-back mandolin. She picked it up and tuned it, saying, "Same as a violin."

Then she played a slow fiddle air. It was beautiful and delicate, and the acoustics of the room made of it an intimate thing. As it began to repeat, she nodded to a four-string tenor guitar hanging nearby. I lifted it carefully off the hook, leaned close to check the tuning, and then plucked out notes as if playing a bass. And the magic timelessness of music and candlelight enwrapped us, taking us out of our bodies, and it seemed we were not just two there but three.

The final notes seemed not to end. Rather, their reverberations diminished in the instruments in our hands and could be perceived to spread through the shop from instrument to instrument, string to string. Like the candlelight, they faded into the ever-deeper shadows, tangibly into the past. Celeste's eyes in that dim light were like those of a nighttime Cheshire Cat, sad and fading.

"Try to get some sleep. Go up now. Don't think. Listen to the music in your head. I can get home in the dark."

She nodded and gave me a brief hug, the mandolin between us, and whispered, "Thank you."

I stepped through the Dickensian door, and the imaginary bell in my head made no sound, for it was muffled in mourning. I turned to see a hand holding a candle gliding slowly toward the back of the shop, its light slipping softly from surface to surface and then disappearing up the stairs.

The night I turned to was different from any I had ever seen in the city, different from what anyone had seen for maybe two hundred years. It was dark, only punctuated occasionally by a building that had a backup power source. The widely spaced lit windows blended with a profusion of stars unseen by modern city dwellers. They came right down to the skyline, silhouetting it and faintly demarking the way home.

Nearly back and lost in thought and musical echoes, I didn't pay much attention when I came to an illuminated storefront. There was a thunking sound that drew my attention. Someone was tapping something on the window from within. Pulled reluctantly from reverie, I looked into the light. A face . . . familiar. Alice was motioning me to come inside, looking concerned.

Hesitant, I did as bid.

She is perceptive; I'll give her that. There would be no dueling tonight, no trying to catch each other out.

She led me to a table in a room that was far from empty of people but strangely hushed in face of uncertainty.

"Hey, what's up? I didn't really notice where I was precisely."

"Clearly." Treading softly, she said lightly, "Charles, it's our pub. You could hurt a girl's feelings by forgetting the spot of our first date."

I looked around. "Oh, geez. Wow, I was seriously in another world. Why are you here?"

She motioned to several battery packs on the table plugged into nearby sockets. "Everyone in here is charging their devices."

I suppose I still seemed disoriented, because she frowned and reached across the table and laid her hand on my forearm. "What?"

So I told her, and she listened, eyes traveling compassionately across my face. When I spoke of the music and the candlelight, she smiled slightly. But when I cycled back and explained the details of the disastrous train of events that resulted in Mr. Lathke's death, her grip tightened on my arm and her eyes went steely.

"I hate that! People think of these things as big, generalized events, but really, they are collections of very real, personal, and often tragic, devastating stories. This is the lesson we should have learned in the last pandemic. Everything is so interconnected, interdependent. It's not enough to strengthen the CDC if we can't keep the power on, the water. And then people, beautiful people like your friend die."

Her face was a shifting mask of compassion and frustration. Her hand slid down to mine, and she gave it a gentle squeeze.

"I'm so sorry for your loss, Charles . . . and of course, Celeste's. I need to go, but I hope to see you . . . well . . . Here, why don't you take one of these battery packs? It'll last you a couple days if necessary. Hopefully the power will be back on soon."

She rose and stepped to the door, tapping my shoulder as she passed. In a few minutes, I left too.

I was in a pretty stripped-down mood, thinking of how blithely the human race steps into the fist of apocalypse. Recurrent cycles of doom: natural disasters of lava, earthquake, tsunami, flood, and typhoon—meteors, for God's sake, the black death. And it's always, "Eat, drink, and be merry," leaving off the last part of the saying, "for tomorrow we die." Of course, living in fear is no good, but don't we ever learn? In times like these, I always think, cynically or realistically, I'm not sure which, there's no problem on earth that can't be solved with the simple expedient of the eradication of the human species. Well, not meteors and volcanoes, of course. But yeah, we make most of our own problems—and many of the earth's—extinction of animal species, the very weather of a vast planet. All of which to say, I don't know how I made it home and into my dark room with its welcoming bed and the mixed relief of unsettled dreams.

Then passed a week in limbo, with less company than Dante envisioned. It was a strange period of anxiety, boredom, hope, confusion, and tedium. Electricity, that element we have come to think of as much a right as water, predictable and as reliable as day, became a fickle and elusive force, like the wind. It would ripple through the neighborhoods like a zephyr, and then fade to nothing, only to roar back, but only for short, unpredictable periods, as engineers and politicians struggled to manage locally generated power from a solar array here, a wind farm there, to give everyone a little bit of the little that could be made and moved around. I imagine that the well-to-do folks in the suburbs were somewhat insulated under their solar panel roofs, if not in terms of goods and services. But the greater, complex web of electricity generation and distribution was dormant.

Rumors and conspiracy theories flew when there was enough passing power for people to briefly vent their frustrations online. Mostly, though, we husbanded our unannounced allotments of electricity, leaping into action when it came at odd hours in the day or night, hoping to get some laundry done or opening the fridge or even doing some work. The college, of course, could not run, but we were enjoined to be ready to spring into action the moment normality reliably returned. I reckon the extroverts managed to cobble together some sort of crippled revels to stave off introspection, but much of the population—ambiverts—was depressed. The real introverts were probably the happiest except when there wasn't enough light to read by . . . so maybe not all that content either.

Anyway, it was a long, blurry week.

It was in this altered, darkened, somber world, in that gloomy mood, and with that scant explanation, that I turned to the old book.

And no, I won't say exactly when I lifted it from Celeste. Let it be a lesson to never completely trust a first-person narrator. Call me a cad, bounder, burglar, defalcator, or what you will, you'll get no argument from me. I had it in my hand, and that's an end to it.

The last time I opened the book, it was little more than an expectant, or ominous, palimpsest, so I turned the cover warily. Not realizing I was holding my breath, I exhaled when I saw text.

The Silent Plague

The great plague scoured the earth. In densely populated areas, it raged like a wildfire, indiscriminate, and in other places, it meandered on the back of a desert caravan or thrust up winding streams in canoes or trekked on foot across mountains or sailed in ships and fishing boats. In this way, the disease took everyone on Earth in its grip, if not in the first fiery circuit, then in one of the slower passes over the course of several years, as it swirled and eddied and renewed itself again and again before finally running out of hosts and going dormant, perhaps forever. Thus, not a soul escaped the ravages of the sickness. But not one died either.

The plague was one that brought about a downy veil of silence that draped the entire globe, for every person living then was struck profoundly deaf. No one could hear a single sound, no matter the volume, the pitch, the timbre. The proverbial tree falling in the forest was silent, but it still fell, and people knew it fell, and that was very troubling. They were aware as never before that the laws of physics were not suspended by their deafness, or even their existence. The treefall still shook the forest and caused animals to cry in alarm. Lightning still split the night and shook their houses, but there was no thunder. No waves seemed to roar against the stony shores below shrieking gulls. Herds of beasts still vibrated the ground with their thousand-hoofed drumming, but all was quiet. One of the most devastating realizations of the people of the world was that though they could still see songbirds, raptors, waterfowl, and all the rest of the avian folk on the wing, in the trees, on the shore, and in fields, as they opened their beaks to call, squawk, and sing, not one sound could be discerned.

And then, tragically, some people began to die. While the world has had deaf people in numbers for all of human history, people who struggled and adapted or were assisted and thrived or didn't thrive, now everyone faced that challenge, and some were not up to it. Some of these succumbed to despair and slipped away, or swam far out into the silent sea until they could swim no more, or used any number of ways to extinguish their lives, for humans are endlessly creative even in the grim task of self-destruction.

Even this was not yet devastating to human civilization, though all the silence on so vast a scale, the complete unpreparedness for other types of communication, did weaken every type of community fabric, from mighty city to hidden village. Then came something more. People came to realize that their very belief systems were crippled. Their deep gatherings and their less deep ones were fractured alike, for the glue that held them together, whether in worship or play, was gone. They could no longer make or hear or move to or laugh at or cry to . . . music. Melody and auditory rhythm, even the ancient sound of hands clapping and lips whistling, were mute.

Then, indeed, the very foundations of the world were shaken in ways that could only be compared to world war or global tsunami or volcanic ash blanketing the planet. People collectively, not just individually—which is a different thing altogether, not just of scale but of social dynamics and practices, politics, economics, and the rest—were not built to circumvent total, universal silence. The survivors would have to remake every type of human interaction and community to accommodate silence. And some, many, most even, set out after a time of chaos and collapse, to do that.

But a kind of despair had been inserted into the human psyche. No one could long forget what was lost when every flitting bird was a reminder. There came a time when, for many people, the mere glimpse of a musical instrument was a kind of torture.

So it came to pass that some of these well-meaning souls determined to remove the painful trigger. They set out to do a difficult thing, a thing they thought necessary if the populace of the entire world were to recover and begin an entirely new era of life on Earth. They began gathering and destroying all the instruments they could find. Of course, they could not find them all, and of course, many pockets of resistance smoldered if only for the nostalgia of music. But many strings, horns, pipes, drums, and all the noisemakers of every type of ensemble were stilled.

It was a cleansing purge to rid the collective consciousness of the beguiling, enigmatic, and irretrievable power of music. The purge was erratic, following along the very paths and arteries the plague had traversed.

In time, people realized that they needed some way to cauterize the wound of the amputation. Something must be planted in the deep soil from which music had been ripped. Again, slowly, haltingly, ultimately, a new nearly as magical a thing as music began to emerge and be promulgated. The Cult of Color.

It was well-chosen and natural, for wasn't sight humankind's first revelation? Along with its fraternal twin, hearing, seeing was the doorway to interacting with and understanding the world. To see was to learn wonder. Think of the multiplicity of form of the natural world: the shapes of the land; the forms of plants and trees; animals of myriad types and color and behavior; the mystery of moving water in streams, waterfalls, and waves; the sky! Yes, the color-shifting tapestry of the sky, always changing and throwing up vast curtains of color and being muted by slanting rain showers, which were then pierced by beams of sunlight. And the culmination of all color magic, the rainbow. Surely it was the first hint humans had received that there might be more, might be somewhere that could make necessary the coinage of a word like *heavenly*. And the stunning leap of imagination to consider the possibilities of gods.

With such a heritage, it was not so difficult a process for sight to reassert its primacy of human senses, thought, and inspiration. Sight was, after all, the source of naming. Humans saw a thing and gave it a name. No, it was not the other way around, as some foolish philosophers claim. That is just vanity. Humankind is not causal; it is observant.

Thus, the Cult of Color gave rise to new uses of color, new expressions, new color tools, ways to share colors, blend them, communicate with them, letting them become the way people spoke, the way they played, the art they created, the concerts they attended. Color became music. It was danced to, for rhythm could still be discerned in pulsating light. People became more and more attuned to subtle hues and often stopped to appreciate some passing shift in the shade of blue in the sky; the endless patterns and grades of greens and blues and browns and golds and grays and violets of moving water; the shades of green, brown, red, and gold in autumnal forests, now in sunlight, now in shade, now rippled with wind, now draped in snow—itself a screen on which was projected a ceaseless variety of color.

Color became a kind of religion, but it was one in which wonder and joy, surprise and pleasure predominated. Thus, it fostered gratitude. People were happy to share a sunset, thrilled to witness the northern lights. Color was good. It was a gift to all humanity, and humanity was collectively wise enough to embrace the gift. So through deep loss came a betterment of human society, one that caused a turning back to the natural kingdom of the world, a desire to be more attuned to it and less enthralled with the material constructions and destructions of the past. And people were brought out of despair and given hope. This, of course, didn't mean that there arose a golden age, a utopian halcyon period. No, there was so much to do to restore the damaged structures of community, of commerce, of governments in country and village, and of global interactions. The vicissitudes of life remained, but it was a struggle made bearable by the consolation of color.

Amid all the work of restructure, rebuilding of lives, and the development and spread of color harmony, it may not be surprising that it took quite a while for something to be noticed. Sound was no longer, could no longer, be attended to. Things that made noise in the past were no longer thought of as having that property. Bird mouths still opened in song, but no one thought of what the open mouths meant. So gradually, they stopped caring and refocused on the beautiful refractions of light in the birds' feathers.

The adults, thus attuned to sight, were late in recognizing that the children born after the pandemic that had, it seemed, forever removed sound from the world were moving their mouths like the birds, even in response to the birds opening their mouths. And the children, siblings, and playmates all were doing it all the time. In all those different cultures and communities across different continents and islands and races, children could hear.

This realization sent shock waves all around the world. It reverberated. It caused upheaval. Sound had returned to humankind! What did that mean for culture? What did that make of all the new communications and appreciation, love even, of color? Would sound reassert dominance in human interaction? Should it be suppressed? Such were the discussions of those who were reminded of their loss and were threatened by the idea that coming generations would treat them as handicapped, as wounded survivors of global catastrophe, while the world of sound left them behind.

They needn't have been quite so worried, because children are malleable and wise. They were growing up with the benefits of the Cult of Color that their wonderfully creative elders had devised. These children were masters of the art of color, having imbibed it from birth. They were better at its myriad manifestations than their parents. And, credit these elders, they saw this and were comforted and rejoiced.

Now adults turned their creative energies toward finding ways to teach the children to use their hearing, to rebirth spoken language. And in every single community across the vast world, there were people who remembered how to make the music they themselves could no longer hear. Many instruments had survived the great purge and were brought out of their hiding places and lovingly restored and duplicated.

In this way, music was reborn in the human family, and in time, music and color were united in new ways unimaginable before.

EIGHTEEN

I recalled that the book seemed to somehow slant the stories to fit the reader. One more mystery about the thing, and I didn't really have the mental acuity after all the inactivity to ponder the implications, but it did kind of remind me of Mr. Lathke's collection of instruments hanging silently in the dark. The story seemed like a dream in the way dreams arise from pieces of life and morph into stories and symbols. But that's as far as I cared to take it. I did think that I might want to share it with Celeste sometime—book-possession complications notwithstanding. So I didn't shut it, merely set it open hanging over the edge of the side table to preserve both the story and the spine of the book. The thought of the instruments led to my own artifact of musical history, the little rajão.

I retrieved the old case and brought out the pretty little instrument. Noodling around on it for a bit was frustrating. I could figure out fingerings and approximate chord shapes, but what I wanted was just one lesson, one observation, especially to actually hear what kind of music this little box had made in its long life.

Maybe there were some "Portagee"—as the little girl's letter had it—musicians somewhere in the region that I could seek out. With my neighborhood being blessed with a dose of electricity, I searched online for some evidence of such folk but came up empty. All I found was reference to a little combination Mexican tienda and music shop. What the heck, it would be a good day to get out of city hibernation and drive east across the bridge. My car had gas, so I didn't bother trying to call, just jumped in with my rajão and headed out in eerily light traffic.

The place was in Walnut Creek, an upscale town nestled in the hills east of the bay. It reminds me of Santa Barbara. Both are lovely towns and maybe a bit more affluent than strictly necessary, if you know what I mean. I parked in the big parking structure downtown and strolled along Olympic and turned down Locust. It was a pleasant walk, and lots of other people must have agreed. I've never seen so many baby strollers. Quite a few restaurants and stores were closed, but as I came to the address I was looking for, there was a hand-lettered sign on the glass door that said, "Trying to Be Open, Come On In." I did.

I'd never been in a place quite like it. Its name was Caldo de Musica, and unless my high school Spanish failed me, I believed it to mean *music soup*. I stood there looking around, taking in the juxtaposition of cozy restaurant and music shop. It was all quite welcoming and tastefully arranged, with tables and booths on one side, and on the other, beyond a small stage, instruments and store counter and practice rooms. Everywhere there were musical instruments and posters, and it smelled great. I must have been gaping, because a man came up to me and looked with raised eyebrows, first at my instrument case and then at my face.

"Welcome. What can I do for you? Food or music, or a bit of both?"

"This is such a cool place. I've never been here before, just found it online, which said something like music tienda."

"So you were expecting something more . . . Mexican?"

That was said with a bit of an edge, and I wondered if out here there was still some lingering ethnic tension. I paused and smiled. "Like the dirt-floored tortilla shop I went to years ago in Baja del Sur. I would like to taste the cornmeal soup I had down there. Never had it since. But no, I came about this." I lifted the case.

The man smiled. “Okay, both it is. I’ll get you a bowl of that very soup and bring it over. Why don’t you sit in the booth closest to the music side? You can put your case on the counter. I’m eager to see what you’ve got inside.”

I did as bid and soon was savoring a taste from the past. I looked across the room at the man, caught his eye, and mouthed, “That’s it,” to which he nodded knowingly and turned back to his work.

When I was done, he came back to clear and said, “That was it, right?”

“Oh my gosh, that taste brought me back to a long, long time ago.”

“I’m glad to hear it. Now about that case. My name is Enrique, by the way.”

“Charles. Pleasure. Yes, let’s get into that.”

We stepped over to the counter, and I opened the case. Enrique’s face took on a look of intense interest, and he slipped into Spanish. “*Dios mío. ¿Que tiene aquí, amigo?* May I pick it up?”

“Of course. Do you know what it is?”

He didn’t answer immediately but lifted the instrument with the tenderness of an art connoisseur, turning it this way and that in the light, looking at the pretty but simple joinery, the straightness of the neck, the patina of the wood on the back.

“If I’m not mistaken it’s old-world, maybe Portuguese, quite old.” He ran his thumb across the strings. “It’s a bit like a ukulele, but . . . hmm.”

He looked speculatively at me. “Where did you get it, if you don’t mind me asking?”

“My friend gave it to me. Mr. Lathke, who . . .”

“You know Mr. Lathke? He gave it to you? Wow! Lathke is a hero around here. Say, are you in a hurry or anything? Do you mind if I call my son? He knows a lot about this stuff, has his doctorate in ethnic musicology.”

"Oh, wow, really? Sure, that would be fabulous. I got nothing goin' on with this electricity thing happening."

"*¡Que bueno!* I'll give him a call. Have a look around, be comfortable. The soup, by the way, is on the house!"

I could hear him on the phone. His perfect English diction slid into a rapid Spanglish, with every third or fourth word being English and the rest Spanish. I always loved hearing it and envied the creative fluidity of the combination of languages.

He returned and announced enthusiastically, "He'll be here shortly. He's excited to see what you have. Hey, are you busy this evening, I mean in a couple hours? We have our monthly music jam in a while."

"No, that sounds super. Like I said, nothing is happening in my world at the moment, and I would be honored to get a glimpse into yours. Thank you."

I walked around Alma Park for a while enjoying the trees and young families and thinking it was a lovely name for a park, *soul*. The Japanese have a practice they call *shinrin-yoku*, forest bathing, spending time among the trees, imbibing the restorative tonic of nature. I felt the tightness of city living ease out of my mind and muscles.

When I returned to Caldo de Musica, it was changing. An interesting cross section of ethnic subgroups seemed to be assembling. They were different in color and clothing, in speech and manner, but they were all merry, and they all were pulling instruments out of cases and packs and gig bags. And these, too, were as varied as the owners, the names of which, owner and instrument, I was to learn as the afternoon progressed. There were the Goldilocks members of the Mariachi family, the little *vihuela Mexicana*, and the monstrous *guitarrón*, along with the Irish cittern, Greek bouzouki, American banjo, Russian balalaika, fiddles, guitars, a Japanese koto, an Indian sitar, and a number of ukuleles of different configurations. I was beginning to see why Enrique might know Mr. Lathke.

I was introduced to Enrique's son, Sebastian, and we had time to briefly look at the rajão, at which he smiled and proclaimed it an old friend. Apparently, he had used it and other exotic instruments from Mr. Lathke's shop for his historical research.

He looked at me quizzically and said, "So he gave to you? He wouldn't part with it when I asked to buy it. Deep one, he is."

From his comments, I could tell he held the old luthier in high esteem, so I felt it appropriate to tell him of his passing and its cause. That froze him, and he was silent for a time. "Do you mind if I mention it to the group? A lot of them know and respect him very, very much. He often came here and was a wonderful friend to el Caldo."

"Okay, well, sure, of course."

With that, he turned and stepped up on the low stage and raised a hand to get the attention of the group, which was now settled in at tables, chairs, booths, and counter, most with instruments perched on laps.

"Welcome to the bowl of music, *bienvenido,* aloha." These and other greetings echoed back in a variety of languages.

"As you all know, we meet here monthly to make music on instruments from around the world and welcome anyone to join us. For the benefit of those who may be new, again welcome. I hope you have a grand time and make some new friends—new people and new music alike."

This received some applause, and he continued, "Now we do have some ground rules that I'll share. They are designed to maximize the variety of music you bring and to respect the ethos of those genres. So we generally go around, and those who choose to suggest a song tell us a bit—a *bit,* I emphasize. No long speeches, friends, we gotta get to the music."

There was a ripple of laughter in the room and some knowing looks.

"Please follow the requests of the person suggesting the song. Some may invite you all to join in and, as our Hawaiian contingent says, I believe, *changalang*, which if I have it right, means *strum along*. Then we'll have the full stew, an Italian cioppino. Others may be playing in a style that is best with just a few, or even a single, instrument. On those, listen and enjoy. We have learned from our friend and mentor Mr. Lathke to hear the nuances of the instruments, the tones, their colors.

"On that note, I'd like to do a couple of things before we start."

"You mean a long speech?" some wag called out to laughter.

Sebastian smiled. "Got me, amigo. First, I want to introduce a new friend to el Caldo and show you his instrument. Charles, bring that case up here will you?"

I did and was warmly welcomed by the group. I turned over the case and retreated to my seat.

Sebastian reverently lifted the rajão out of the case and held it up, rotating it so all could see it. "Anyone know what this is?"

There were a number of guesses, but no one got it right. Sebastian looked my way. "Charles, what's it called, and where did you find it?"

"It's a rajão, from the Portuguese island of Madeira. It is the precursor to the ukulele." That brought excited whispers from the uke players. "And it was given to me by my friend Mr. Lathke."

This brought even more exclamations.

Sebastian then stepped in. "And now for my little speech, a disquisition, if you will, on the origin and influence of this humble music box, which I hope will not be overlong, but enlightening."

Again, there were chuckles, and he preceded to explain the history very much in the way it had been told to me. I glanced over at the ukulele folks, and they were enthralled in learning the genealogy of their instrument.

At the end of his explanation, there was a light round of applause that died away as the audience took in the somber expression on Sebastian's face.

"And now, friends, I'm afraid it is my duty to convey to you more news that I learned from Charles. It seems that dear old Mr. Lathke, whose first name none of us learned, old-world gentleman that he . . . was. Yes, he has passed from this world into whatever is beyond . . . and if the universe is at all just . . . into a realm of heavenly music."

The room was as still and silent as can be, for tears make no sound.

"One more thing I'll pass on, though I suppose it's unnecessary. He died of the coronavirus."

This was met with gasps, exclamations, and questions. He raised his hand for quiet. "He couldn't take the vaccine, and as we have all learned, these things never really go away. So let's take a moment to reflect on the many gifts Mr. Lathke brought to our corner of the musical world and offer up such thoughts and prayers to such deities as may grace the cultures you represent."

The silence again was profound, and I had the sense that the feelings about our lost friend were made more poignant by the painful memories from not so long before of the terrible pandemic that had struck so deeply and indiscriminately into the lives of everyone on Earth. For myself, I realized then that this repressed emotion was the source of the disquiet that I had been feeling during the blackout.

After some time, Sebastian resumed. "Now friends, I suspect Mr. Lathke would chide us for being too morose and hasten us to music. So let's dedicate our playing tonight, be it melancholy or humorous or anything between, to him. I suggest we start with the Hawaiian uke group. Take us into song!"

A fellow stood up, ukulele in hand and said, "Ho, *brah*, can sing one *mele lidat, kanikapila kine* style—for you *haole* folks, that means everybody may play along and sing it if you know it. An' mebbee auntie dance one hula *foah* send our aloha to Kumu Lathke. *'Wahine Ilikea,' geev'um."*

He sat and nodded and suddenly everyone was strumming. A guitar had appeared as if by magic in my hands, so I followed the left hand of another guitar player and listened, trying to hear what a balalaika or koto or *guitarrón* sounded like playing Hawaiian music. Then a lovely older lady stood and called out a Hawaiian word, and the singers came in on the first verse starting with that word. She began dancing in a most graceful way, apparently in partial pantomime of the words. This was hula as I had not seen it, deeply melodic, haunting, and affecting. Between verses, she called out the cue to the next verse. Everyone played gently, sang sweetly, and was collectively carried by the stream of music.

The music continued for several hours, leaping from style to style, culture to culture, embraced and appreciated by all. Sebastian showed me around the neck of the rajão, and as the sun began to go down into the uncertainties of manmade illumination, we departed, refreshed, united, moved, and if any were like me, changed.

NINETEEN

The power stuttered off and on for the next few days, but there was enough to allow for sudden scampering into kitchens for the brewing of coffee, without which there would have been chaos in the streets! Seriously, we all limped along, though occasionally I would hear or read of something tragic caused by faulty power, or of people's misguided efforts to jury-rig some appliance or cooking apparatus, or even of shutdowns of various municipal functions. One scare had to do with the massive sewage-treatment system, but most were poignant personal tragedies that again opened the thin scar tissue of the myriad pandemic traumas that were not so very far in the past. It made me think of how permanently people had been traumatized by the worldwide Spanish flu pandemic of 1918 that had so tragically swept the stunned survivors of the unimaginable destruction and suffering of World War I. That dreadful illness was spoken of for decades. So here in our inconvenient loss of electricity, nothing by comparison, we were reminded of the caprices of existence and wounds we'd thought healed.

Thus, when power was restored, there was relief, celebration of return to routine . . . and anger. But the celebratory aspects dominated the news, as businesses large and small alike scrambled to get back up to speed. This, of course, included the college, and I was soon nose to grindstone preparing to redeem the somewhat truncated semester.

One news item I could not ignore, for it was trumpeted repeatedly, was the heroic rescue and reorganization of the electric grid across the country by a company called ApolloNet. It appeared that they had been given virtual dominion over every aspect of production, distribution, and sale of electricity in the country, from traditional to experimental, from locally distributed to satellite controlled. It was a virtual monopoly on a scale unseen since the days of the early 1900s, bestowed by an appreciative Congress, who were happy to trade deregulation for promises of reliability, huge profits for reelection prospects, and entrance to the exclusive club of industry titans for enhanced power. It looked like Ray and Maurice had made it into the proverbial smoke-filled back rooms where the elite made policy, and money and access joined hands. I wondered if the boys had taken up golf, as so much wheeling and dealing seemed still to happen on the course. Not that I knew. Maybe I'm just spouting the old populist line, grousing about fat cats. They did get my electricity back on, so what should I care? I was as happy as most to stop thinking about the past. I did, however, reflect often on my experience at Caldo de Musica, and I suspected there was more to be learned there, and not just about how to play my rajão.

A few days later, after a productive morning being an academic, I was feeling like I often do at the beginning of a semester. That is to say, though many schools and universities, being completely online, no longer had traditional semesters, the breaks between ours were still long enough that instructors could indulge in different personae and activities in the interim. Thus, it can be a jolt to return to work. However, after a while of prep and engagement, we—I, anyway, remember what I am about, my craft, as it were, and become again a competent and enthusiastic practitioner, my perpetual cynicism notwithstanding.

It was a very pretty Northern California early afternoon, bright and clear with neither sea breeze, rain, nor fog. I decided to reward myself for my honest work and take a long walk. I thought that by way of destination I would go across to Mr. Lathke's—Celeste's now—shop and check on her. The walk, though, the calm air, clear sky, and vivid colors of tree and garden along the way were the main draws, their gaiety likely more refreshing than Celeste's mourning mood in the darkened old atelier.

When I walked up, that expectation was thrown. The front door was propped open, shades were drawn up, and lights were blazing. More surprising, there was laughter coming from within. I stepped in from the bright sunlight into the unfamiliarly bright shop and stood for a moment a bit dazzled. Two voices, male and female, called out together, "Charles!"

My eyes adjusted, but I must have had an odd look on my face, because they both laughed. It was just so unexpected, the bright shop, the cheerful mood, and waving me in, Celeste and Sebastian.

Recovering, I stepped in. "What cheer, amigos?"

Celeste smiled. "You're mixing cultural idioms, Charles. But welcome; you're just in time to help!"

"What's goin' on in here? I've never been in here with it so light! Thought I was in the wrong place."

I went over, kissed her on the cheek, and shook Sebastian's hand. "Good to see you again. I sure enjoyed el Caldo the other night. What a marvelous group. And thanks again for teaching me about my little instrument. That kind of shook the dust off it, made it come alive for me."

"It was a genuine pleasure to see it again and make your acquaintance. I hope you'll come again."

"I thought I would tell Celeste about it, but I see you two already know each other."

She chimed in, "How could we not? This guy haunted this shop talking to my dad for hours and hours about arcane instrument stuff, culture, musicology. Dad could hardly get rid of him!"

We laughed and she continued, "Since Dad gave some of his prized instruments away to . . . uh . . . worthy . . . recipients, like you, me, a museum here, a collector there . . . even Sebastian got a sweet little flamenco guitar . . ."

He smiled and picked up the thread. "Sweet indeed, old, and . . . well, not to go off on one of my disquisitions, we thought we should do a careful inventory of what's left and update and digitize these."

He pointed at the table around which we were standing. It was covered with neat file folders, some opened, revealing lists of instruments and what appeared to be detailed notes about them. These were being transcribed, while every instrument was located, checked, and evaluated, adding to the description. It was clearly a big job.

They explained their method to me, and I found a role retrieving instruments and finding and matching their documentation while Sebastian examined them, making fresh notes and Celeste entered all the data into a mobile terminal.

We were a diligent and merry crew, stopping often to handle and attempt to play the instruments from around the world, making observations about them, while Sebastian gave the occasional short disquisition about them.

In this way, the afternoon passed, and eventually I decided I would drift home. We said friendly farewells, and as I slipped out the door, I glanced back to see their heads together as they looked closely at a mandolin, laughing.

I was barely in the door when I received a text message from Alice which read, "In desperate need of alcohol, red meat, and friendly company. Pub?"

Bemused by the repeated juxtaposition, I wrote back, "Okay, when?"

"Whenever, I'm on my way now."

"Okay, walking out the door."

I headed back to the sidewalk choosing to have no expectations, having been so wrong earlier. Instead, I thought about the linguistic shifts between standard written language and text messages: the breakdown of rules of grammar, degrees of formality, and such within informal discourse subgroups. A pretty tired subject these days, perfect for the small task of tamping down my curiosity.

We arrived outside If the Shoe Fits simultaneously. I involuntarily stopped and surveyed her face.

She grimaced and brushed by, holding a hand up to the near side of her face. "I know, I look a wreck. Come on, I need beer!"

She led me inside, and it being early, the place was almost empty, so we had our pick of tables. She went to the back where there were a few little alcoves lined with bookshelves and tables with very comfortable chairs. My kind of old-fashioned, cozy spot.

"I didn't see these tables when we were here before. Reminds me of my virtual library."

"No sparring tonight, Charles."

She flopped down, tossed her pack on another chair, and theatrically closed her eyes and exhaled. A waitress appeared instantly, and before she could even ask, Alice said, "I could go for a nice tall Guinness."

"Make it two, please."

Shortly, the glasses appeared, and we raised them in salute and took a long, appreciative pull. That's the thing about beer; it allows you to quaff in a way you never can with wine or spirits: profligate and thirst-quenching.

"I imagine work has been intense recently with all this electricity and government stuff . . ."

"No, you can't imagine it. It's beyond all power of imagination. The organization, the negotiations, the politics, the finances, the technical . . . unbelievable. And to have to navigate, mollify, shepherd, even comprehend the weird interactions of my two bosses. I'll tell you this . . . those guys are not on the same page. The tension in that place. I feel like I'm working two or three jobs. But enough of that—too much of that. I'm famished. I need some kind of massive protein infusion."

We ordered some of the giant house special bacon, avocado, and grilled onion burgers and gorged and gulped in the otherwise silent alcove.

It was lovely. We were comfortable, even companionable, just sharing a simple indulgence of burgers and stout without really talking. It was like putting a racing engine in neutral and just coasting . . . revving down.

Halfway through a second glass, we were stuffed and a little tipsy, glad to be in comfortable chairs apart from the gradually filling pub. Alice had taken off her glasses, and she looked over at me through tired eyes, smiled, and sighed. She made ready to speak and then lapsed back into silence, as if not wanting to pick up the heavy weight of matters of consequence, as the Little Prince put it.

So I told her about the Caldo de Musica, the little details of the evening, the varied participants. I lingered on my impressions of the hula, both the song and the dance, the idea of multiple generations sharing the spirit of the song about a woman's hair that is like a waterfall, about how the seemingly trite word *aloha* was thus freshly imbued with rich, multifaceted meaning. I told her about learning to play my rajão and how Mr. Lathke had given it to me and its origins, and about learning how he had been a kind of respected mentor to this diverse set of musicians. And I told her about Sebastian and the cataloging of the instruments in the shop and of Celeste's telling stories about them earlier, and it all seemed of a piece, one unified story with some ineffable thread linking the elements. All the while, Alice listened, sometimes with eyes closed as if to visualize what I was describing, sometimes looking at my face, sometimes taking tiny sips from her glass.

Finally, my story reached its end and guttered like a spent candle. The silence was gradually replaced by the convivial din of a nearly full pub. It seemed like we had been in a bubble that had now dissolved.

Alice stirred, polished off her drink, put on her glasses, and sighed as if reluctant to return to the world.

"Thank you, Charles. That was exactly what I needed . . . better than I hoped. I gotta press on . . . a few things to take care of before bed . . . though perhaps I should take a cab home." She smiled in self-depreciation. "More than I normally drink, Professor."

"You okay?"

"Oh yeah. I feel so much better. I'm gonna grab this check. Little enough for the lovely therapy session."

She stood and made to go and then leaned forward a little. "Oh, by the way, ApolloNet is having a big celebration, with all the company and politicians and staff—a gala, I guess. You should come."

I raised skeptical eyebrows.

"Yeah, I know, not your kind of thing nor your kind of people, but I want you to come. You'll find it entertaining if nothing else. Please do come. I'll send you one of the engraved invitations . . . suitable for framing!"

With that she laid a hand on my shoulder, turned, and left.

TWENTY

A few days later, the invitation did arrive. It was, indeed, engraved. A fortnight more and I was as dressed up as an English professor can get, which I must insist is a good deal beyond the dubious splendor of the stereotypical tweed jacket. It was no tux, though, and as I made my way into the ballroom, I saw that the tuxedo was well-represented. Of course, though, it was the women who shone. One might have thought he had stumbled into a Hollywood opening, all bright gowns, flashing jewels, upswept hair, and down-swept necklines. My inner snob rose to the fore, perhaps only in self-defense. I wondered for the thousandth time how women can work so hard, for so long, to be treated as more than chattel, and then exert so much effort to make of themselves virtual displays of sexual objectification, challenging men to look at their bodies as nothing less than a triumph of the seductive arts. No, I say to the protest; it is not simply freedom of self-expression and style. That way lies sophistry.

Suffice to say, I was not thrilled to be there. These kinds of events—not, I admit, that I'd been to many—seem to try so hard to ape some ethos of chic glamour, style, and especially, casual wealth. It just comes across as good old nouveau riche ostentation. Okay, I was in a sour mood. People in the teaching profession never like to be reminded that society undervalues their contribution.

"Is that a scowl on your face, Charles?"

Right in front of me stood, I admit, a lovely, small woman: Alice. She was dressed in what appeared to be black silk, a kind of elegantly flowing yet simple jacket and pants ensemble. No jewelry except for some onyx earrings that barely showed at the edge of her similarly simple hairstyle. Now here, I thought, was an image that conveyed the right combination of feminine elegance and strength, highlighting her intelligent eyes. Her mien was that of confidence and sophistication, not really different than her usual affect except in degree.

"Sir, you are looking at me speculatively. I'm not sure whether to be flattered or offended."

Her impish smile was in evidence, and I loosened up. "Oh, sorry, I was just judging all these glammed-up show ponies and found your attire refreshingly attractive and appropriate."

"Oh dear, are you a bit of a prude, Professor?"

"Hardly, ma'am, I would simply rather not be forced to gaze deeply into every décolletage in the room. Better, wouldn't you say, modern woman that you are, to have a man at least start with eye contact?"

"Nobly put, but did I not observe your eyes traversing my entire form?"

"Indeed, I was noticing the elegant sweep and flow of the silk, as if it were moving in a light zephyr."

We both burst into laughter.

"That's more like it. Moroseness is not the best entrance to a gala. Come in, grab a glass of champagne. You can mingle a bit, or move your judging station to a less conspicuous position. You'll find your seat for dinner at the table over there toward the front . . . by me. I need to be about a few of my zillion duties but will see you in a bit."

She touched my arm, a gesture I was beginning to recognize, and flowed away.

Speaking of triumphant, that pretty well described Ray, though it was mixed with a hefty dose of smugness. He blessed me with fifteen seconds while sweeping around the room being congratulated and generally fawned over, playing the hero.

"Ah, our esteemed professor. Come to rub shoulders with the doers and shakers?"

"Oh, yeah, Ray, got it in one. Ain't you in clover!"

"I'll say. No help from you or my dear ex-girlfriend. But hey, all's fair in love and war . . . especially when you win, right?"

Then he continued on with what seemed to be, in his head, a royal progress through his kingdom. I gulped champagne.

Dinner was good, as these kinds of things go. I sat with Alice, but she seemed distracted and stressed. When her eyes met mine, she smiled, but they quickly sheared off to dart about the room, as if updating an inventory.

Up at the head table, I noticed Maurice next to a generically beautiful mannequin. He, too, was looking smug, but he kept shooting poorly veiled daggers at his business partner. At a guess, I'd have said that Ray had bested him in whatever machinations that had been required to get the monopoly on electricity. Also at that table were several titans of industry as well as the city mayor, a couple state legislators, and our federal senator. All these guys, too, had that air of smug success, like they had pulled off some massive coup that they personally benefited from, but played as if they were magnanimous, self-sacrificing laborers in the fields of community service.

What accompanied dessert—baked Alaska—was the de rigueur procession of set-piece speeches, laced with enough platitudes and false modesty to sink another *Titanic*. It was certainly more than enough to cause most of we poor folk "below the salt" to pour somewhat freely from the bottles of whites and reds placed plentifully around our tables. Free food and drink are the consolations of such stultifying confabulations. They certainly give the men a glib, faux charm, which they imagine the over—or under—dressed women must find delightfully sexy. Thus titillated, it was easy to ignore the rhetorical flourishes from the podium, though interestingly, everyone was still able to applaud on cue. *Most,* I thought, *must practice.*

Maurice did not speak, but everyone else up there did, male and female, excepting the several mannequins, who had become strangely invisible. Ray was techie and pompous, dropping names right and left and trying not to claim all the credit. The politicians' speaking styles appeared somehow linked to their levels of ascendency on the political ladder. They exhibited increasingly saccharine levels of bonhomie mixed with noblesse oblige, none more so than the good senator, who waxed poetically about his spearheading and lobbying efforts in successfully passing the required deregulation and attendant laws permitting the granting of ApolloNet's unprecedented and complete control of so major and multifaceted an industry.

During all this, Alice had remained conspicuously teetotal and got gradually more agitated, looking around the room and back toward the entrance to the hall. Finally, there was a commotion back there, and a large group began entering.

A loud voice called out, "Please give me your attention! We are the FBI. We need you to remain seated and silent."

Consternation was universal, and it was far from silent. The senator at the microphone, with unflappable ease, reiterated the instructions and returned to his seat next to Ray. They whispered rapidly, but the FBI man in charge was again speaking. "Please stay where you are. Agents will be coming around taking your personal information and setting up interviews as deemed necessary."

I turned toward Alice to see how she was reacting, but she was pulling something out of her purse. She stood, gave me a steely, game-face look, touched me again on the shoulder, then slipped a dark-blue windbreaker on over her silk and strode toward the man in charge.

On the back of her jacket were emblazoned the large, recognizable letters: FBI.

At this point, there was an exclamation of outrage from the head table. The senator was trying to mollify Ray, who was loudly twisting away and moving toward the agents, who stiffened.

Ray was yelling, "What the hell is this about! You have no right to disturb this gathering. Get out now!"

He was brought up short as he was suddenly confronted by a diminutive, yet powerful figure: Alice.

He sputtered, "You! You're FBI? A spy, an informer? A traitor!"

He made to push her, and in a flurry, she had his arms pinioned behind his back and was speaking up to his head above her, "Sir, we can do this quietly or not, but you are under arrest for a variety of federal and state offenses." He was incredulous while she stated his Miranda rights. Seeing things under control, the rest of the agents fanned out into the room, several heading to the senator and other public officials.

Then, there was another loud disturbance at the door, a keening female voice followed by surprised voices of warning. I saw a woman push past the awkwardly placed agents around the tables. It was Celeste—furious, shouting something, making a beeline toward . . . Ray, who took an involuntary step backward. The rest of the room was frozen in tableau.

She swept up a bottle as she passed a table and practically ran up to him. "You son of a bitch! You murdered my father!"

She swung the bottle and clocked him right above his eye with a sickening thud and crash as the bottle broke on the floor. He went down into the glass and wine, and the agents sprang into action. Alice was there first and, again with remarkable dexterity, spun Celeste around and had her hands bound in a trice.

The rest happened in a stunned anticlimax: the paramedics wheeled Ray out while Maurice, the senator, and those of his ilk, along with other players I didn't recognize, and also Celeste, were all being led out.

Finally, the remainder of the attendees of this memorable event, having been duly recorded, were allowed to go.

Alice appeared by my side. She had a post-cathartic look about her. We stood looking at each other for a moment.

Once more, she reached out with her characteristic touching of arm and tried to smile. "You will have loads of questions, no doubt, and I hope I can give you satisfactory answers to all of them. In the meantime, would you mind following me down to the office? I'd like to slip Celeste out of the report. There's plenty of big fish being fried, and with all she's gone through . . . Do you mind?"

I did as asked, and all I really remember was dropping Celeste at home. All she had said on the way home was, "I hope I didn't kill the bastard." That and, "Thanks, Charles."

Then I went home with a burgeoning headache.

TWENTY-ONE

The new semester had begun, and it was a very busy time getting it all going. I remember when online education started and we all thought it would be run more or less on autopilot. Some instructors did set up courses that way, and besides the teaching being little better than old-fashioned workbooks, there was considerable resentment from more conscientious professionals about the disparity of workloads for similar pay. And of course, had that model persisted there would be little justification for more than a handful of teachers whose courses could be replicated and run automatically. That sense of self-preservation led to impressive and creative methods to deliver rigorous content. In doing so, we found ourselves spending more rather than less time in myriad forms of interaction with our students.

All of which to say, I was only marginally keeping abreast of the scandal surrounding ApolloNet, and that just from various news outlets, though there was plenty to be read. Apparently, the situation was very bad indeed. Grand juries had been sitting for some time, investigations had been ongoing, wiretaps conducted, money tracked to offshore accounts, elected officials and business leaders bribed and bullied, and as I did have some personal knowledge of, undercover agents placed. There were dozens of arrests. The scope of the web of malfeasance was stunning, as the nature of the electric network reached into every city, business, and household, even into the satellite network. I was reminded, too, that ApolloNet had started out in internet management, so all that was intricately involved as well.

What struck a lot of observers was that the illegality need not have happened. That was driven by greed to take over so many technical aspects of infrastructure and in a hurry. This led to all the opportunities for graft on so many levels: massive kickbacks and bribes had been underway for who knows how long. But the need to update, even universalize many of these systems was real. And the expertise of Ray and Maurice's team was unparalleled. They could have colored within the lines and accomplished much of what they attempted, less completely, more slowly, and less lucratively certainly, but they wouldn't have landed in jail, which is where many involved were headed. Megalomania and hubris, the old tragic flaws in modern dress, had strutted their moment on stage once more and once more had been brought low. People really should read the classics.

The real sticking point, I learned with some dismay, was that ApolloNet had rewritten all the computer code that ran all this stuff. It was proprietary and held close within the company. Were the company to be shut down, the entire massive network would go dark. It was alleged that the blackout had been a warning to politicians, blackmail, as it were—a taste of the disaster ApolloNet could unleash had complete control not been ceded to them.

Thus, the entire country, every person and profession, including mine, was still held up for ransom by the very people hauled in by the Feds, not just Ray et al. but all those elected and nonelected officials, the operators of subsidiaries who had been co-opted in large or innocuous ways, all the people who pulled the levers of this complex machinery. That may have been the most impressive accomplishment of ApolloNet, the massive organizational chart, the key moving parts, use what metaphor you will, it was an enormous undertaking.

And so, what to do next was a very troubling question indeed. Must immunities be granted in order to keep the system going?

After a couple weeks of this firestorm, with almost daily bombshells revealing the magnitude of the corruption, showing us the precipice we collectively stood on, I got a message from Alice requesting my presence at the field office. Well, let me tell you, there are few things as chilling as getting an invitation from the FBI.

I presented myself at the reception desk and waited to be taken to some stark interview room like in the movies. After only a few minutes, Alice wheeled around the counter and walked purposefully up to me.

"Charles, thanks for coming. I hope I didn't scare you with asking you down."

"Well, I was afraid you had unearthed that string of bank robberies I committed in my youth with my gun moll."

"Oh, that, no worries, statute of limitations."

"Whew, was afraid I was gonna get the chair. But I imagine you are busy, so . . ."

"Yeah . . . um . . . let's go upstairs to the canteen. They have decent coffee these days."

I followed her up a flight of stairs into an airy little cafeteria. We each got a cup of coffee—*French roast,* I thought. *This ain't granddad's FBI!* But I held my tongue. Time for banter was over.

At a table by a window overlooking the parking lot, we sat and marshaled our thoughts, sipping the comforting brew.

"How's Celeste? Have you seen her, or . . ."

"Not since that night, and even then, we didn't talk. I mean, she said she hoped she didn't kill Ray, which seemed good, considering."

"Yes, that's a relief. I'm pretty sure she's well out of it. I know she's been somewhat volatile in the past, so least said, best."

"I'm glad to hear it."

Then there was silence into which she eventually said, "Listen, Charles, I asked you down for a couple reasons—one personal, the other professional. Um . . . well, first I want to just say that . . . well . . . yes, as you know I was playing a role—undercover and all—and you know, snooping in your files and some other stuff—that lunch we had, were all part of that, the investigation, trying to figure out how far all this went, who was involved . . ."

She looked up from her cup at which she had been looking while speaking, trying to read my reaction. For no real reason other than I didn't know where all this was going, I remained neutral. She looked down again and continued. "After that, it was clear that you were . . . hmm . . . let's say, on the side of the angels, so I started to consider you a friend. I think you felt that too, though I realize you were wary of me early on too, not unreasonably. Anyway, I hope we can be friends now that the case is out in the open and disguises are off and all that. I know there's still a lot more to clear up, but I wanted to start there before I slip back into my FBI costume."

She looked up again, and I was genuinely surprised to see vulnerability in her expression. I immediately wanted to comfort her. I seemed to suddenly understand something of the enormous strain she must have been under during these past months. I reached across, using her gesture, and touched her forearm.

I smiled and said, "Well, Alice, since you bought me this lovely coffee."

She threw her head back and laughed out loud, tossing my hand from her arm. "I take it back! You are on the side of the demons!"

We both laughed, and the tension evaporated.

"Okay, whew, I'm glad we got through that. Thank you. So switching gears, I want to fill you in on a few details and, actually, thank you on behalf of the Federal Prosecutor's Office."

"Huh?"

"I don't really understand your part in all this, and I don't have to.

Maybe you'll explain it to me sometime, but you really helped the case."

"I did? How in the world did I do that?"

"That book, more specifically that story. You remember when Maurice had you come in to talk about it?"

"Yeah, of course, but—"

"Well, as his PA, he had me scan and transcribe the story. After that and your talk with him, he was different. It was like he was torn about what the company was doing, like for the first time he had an attack of conscience. He started dragging his feet on the plan, fighting with Ray. You heard part of that argument in the office that day. He even yelled out something about the senator. That was a real clue for me. Before that, I wasn't sure about the degree of bribery, and of course that was when Celeste came in and grabbed the book. Well, that was a real surprise. I just didn't get what was so significant about the book. I still don't really. I'm missing something, but it's not important to the case, so it just falls into the category of things I hope you'll explain to me over another tall Guinness. But what I do know is this. When Maurice had me transcribe the story, I had it in my possession for two days. I see that surprises you. So I took it home, well, not home. I brought it here and had forensics analyze it. Why, I don't really know. It just felt so fishy, the way those two guys and you acted around it. So the tech guys looked at it and were really impressed. It's really an ingenious little device. The idea, I guess, came from Celeste's thesis where she postulates some magic little book that tells fresh stories every time it's opened."

She looked at me, and I nodded in confirmation.

"So you and, I reckon, some tech-wizard colleague built one. It's really quite a nifty thing. Am I right?"

"Dead on."

"Okay, but why?"

"It was a kind of experiment really. I wondered if I could influence those guys somehow, you know, ethically, but talking was like a brick wall. So I kind of sold them on the reality of the book. They had known about Celeste's obsession with the idea, and Ray, especially, had sort of bought into the possibility that if something like that could exist, then he should have it, somehow turn it to his own use. I know it sounds crazy now, but even the facsimile we made has enough mystery about it to touch on that ineffable desire most of us have for something more, something not quite believable, something that restores our childhood belief in magic. I don't know if that is a satisfactory answer, and you are right that there's more that lies outside this current situation, but, yeah, maybe over a beer . . . But I still don't get why I am being thanked."

"Because of your ingenious little prank, Maurice got sloppy, which helped us. He also was resisting some of Ray's worst ideas, and that, too, opened some cracks for us to peer into, and now, because he's out on bail pending what looks to be a devastating conviction, he has decided to make a deal and spill all of it. And that's all because you read him perfectly and gave his conscience a surgical jab. His testimony will unravel everything, and believe me it's a very, very tangled skein. So again, sincerely, professionally, and personally, thank you so much!"

I returned home and tried briefly to process all I had seen, heard, and done since I had first stepped into that little musical instrument repair shop. I guess Plato was right: music can be dangerous. That's about as far as I cared to take it at the moment. I was actually relieved to have an engaging job to do. It was fairly complex, intellectually stimulating, and I was doing some good in the world. The intricacies of intrigue and ambition, unappealing in the best of times, looked all the more tawdry in the ugly light of recent events. I prefer it distilled into smoother, but no less true for that distillation, literature.

TWENTY-TWO

I know that at this point in my memoir, I could turn to the undoubtedly entertaining and convoluted legal maneuverings, revelations, and arguments, making of the story a courtroom procedural, but no, that's not for me. Besides, all that complexity would take years of glacial movement before rendering what would seem to many as unsatisfactory justice. Just hearing how the lawyers were setting things up, characters turning on one another, the continued dependence on ApolloNet to run the complex system, the closing of ranks of implicated elected officials and their business cronies. It was as much as I cared to take at the remove of reading news summaries and the occasional opinion piece. The spinning out of such large scandals takes the perspective of years to fully understand, and frankly, I'd had my fill. So back into the ivory tower for me, the door firmly shut.

Shut but not barred, for some weeks later, I received a message from Celeste saying she would like to stop by one afternoon. *Afternoon,* I thought. *Interesting choice.* No wine and candlelight, then. Well, that was fine with me. I imagined there was a fair amount of personal regrouping to be done by anyone concerned in *l'affaire du livre.*

She came, we sat in our places of old, and sipped coffee instead of wine in the bright afternoon sunlight that angled through the window.

I didn't know what to say that wouldn't sound banal, so I waited for her to begin. It was her meeting.

She saw that we would not be easing in through the door of small talk, so she drew breath and set out on her speech. "Okay . . . where to begin. I feel a little nervous, if you can believe that. The woman who wields fists and wine bottles. As you may imagine, there has been plenty of time—and reason—for self-reflection. I clearly need to turn a corner. I have been involved—obsessed is the right word—with that book, my family association with it, my academic work . . . all that stuff stemming from my Uncle John's quite dubious gift. He bequeathed more than the book, as he had certainly come to devote much of his life to the mystery. I see now that he had become . . . I don't know . . . like Bilbo Baggins and the ring . . . and I suppose that would make me Frodo. Not to push the metaphor too hard, but you get my meaning no doubt.

"So it is clearly important for me to let go . . . of everything associated with that crazy, inexplicable book. And somehow that includes in some way my dad's shop . . . and for now . . . you. I know you have, very wisely, pulled back. I have been crazed. Maybe sometime in the future . . . well, one step at a time. No, please don't try to say something comforting. Let me get through this. I have decided that to cut all ties would be a cure as bad as the disease. I need to . . . um . . . transmute the prime elements into something new and clean, alchemy of a sort. So here's what I am thinking. Money is not an object. It hasn't been since Uncle John died. He must have recognized that the book would wreck my life, so gave me the financial means to carry on his obsession. How's that for immortality?

"Well, now I have a plan. I don't have details filled in, because I want to allow for serendipity, but I want to step out on a restorative journey, figuratively but also literally. I am going to go to Spain and try to hike the Camino de Santiago. Going on pilgrimage, I am. Ha, well, I will do it well-equipped and take as long as it seems right. I have been reading about it. So many people walk the Camino for so many reasons, many not religious at all. Personal reasons, breast cancer survivors, midlife crises, some kind of desire for spiritual awakening, or to encounter people from around the world, a community of souls. That and more. It seems appropriate."

She held up a hand to forestall any comment that might come from me, but I was still speechless. I knew there was more coming.

"I am leaving the shop and all that's in it in the, at least temporary, care of Sebastian. He will make suggestions as to what should become of all that. I don't want to be tied to my father's obsessions either. I will be taking the inventory, notes, and images of all the instruments, though. So here's the alchemy part. I want to write. I want to make my own stories, create my own collection of stories. Like the little rajão you were given, every instrument in the shop has its own story, its past, its journey. We've touched on the idea before. Using my notes, and my own imagination, my own creativity, I want to tell their stories, to put together a cycle of short stories that come out of my father's atelier. You see? I want to make something new, something my own, but from the elements of the things—the loves, if you will—that I have inherited. That's the alchemy I am talking about."

She paused, and I thought she had never looked so calm, centered, and appealing in her feline way as sitting there in the overstuffed chair in the shaft of sunlight.

A shadow passed across her face, and she resumed speaking. "And I want to return this to you." She reached into her bag and pulled out an old-looking book, and my heart clenched. "Alice was very kind to me when I could so easily have been arrested. I sense that she is a compassionate person, but also, she was motivated by wanting to act in accordance with what might be your wishes to protect me. I'm not sure, but I am grateful to you both. She visited me, you know, at home, just checking up on me. That was sweet of her. She assumed I knew everything, so she let slip about this."

She held the book up.

"You did a really great job on it, Charles. Had me completely fooled. I was hurt when I learned the truth, but now I see that you were wise to act alone. You did influence the outcome of events . . . in much the way we had learned from that story we read about dividing the brothers. So, well, bravo. Anyway, I want you to have it—and please let's not even talk about the real book. It's calling me right now from one of your bookshelves, probably hiding in plain sight. Maybe you should just destroy it. But that's all I will say on the matter. But there is another thing I want to mention, to thank you for, okay, two things. The first is the stories in your fake book. They are lovely. You are a good writer, Charles, and I encourage you to do more of it. Besides, what's an English professor who doesn't write . . . who doesn't understand the process, the wrestling with creativity, the painting with words? So, Charles, please write more stories. That one I read to you, *The Immortal Song*, was yours?"

"I had some help with the opening, but yes, in the main, it's mine. Some of your alchemy, I suppose."

"I see . . . I think. Just be careful about using the stories in the book. I believe that's what Uncle John did, and he never placed a single one."

"I suspect that to be the case, as well. Don't worry, my—our—training instills a loathing for plagiarism."

"Maybe you can write the story of the book—as a story, as opposed to nonfiction, just as I will be doing with the instruments. And maybe when we are both ready with manuscripts in hand, we can start a little publishing house called something like Uncle John's Books.

"The other thing is . . ." Sunlight made golden tracks of the tears across her cheeks. "Thank you for everything, for putting up with and contributing to my mad escapades. Thank you for our memorable and beautiful trip to Oregon . . ." She ran out of words and didn't see me cross over to her and pull her up into my arms. She sobbed in a way that I thought she hadn't since she was very young, one of those cleansing cries. My eyes were not immune.

After a long moment of this intimate sadness, for what had been and what might have been, she pulled back, smiled, and sat again.

"One last thing, my friend . . . I have taken my first tentative step on my pilgrimage. I have tried to write, or at least start, the first story. May I read it to you . . . not for constructive criticism . . . just to share?"

"Of course, Celeste. I would love to hear it."

A Tale from the Old Music Shop

If it had eyes, it could tell of all it had seen in its long life. If it had a memory, it could tell of its youth, of its long travels. If it could sleep, it would slumber and wake refreshed. It had none of these attributes; however, it did have a heart, and its heart was music. Furthermore, music, in ways unfathomable, has all of those qualities and more. Music lives and touches and travels and sees into places in the human heart that humans themselves cannot see.

Now, though, the old violin hung mute on the wall of the darkened atelier among an elderly cohort of wooden boxes that each in their own way had vibrated and amplified sounds, had sung in their many voices the music of many lands. All was still in the shop; no string moved, no sounds were emitted. If all were personified, what conversations they might have had. But it is as well that they did not have human language, for the language they did possess was far superior to words. Still, the old man whose shop it was knew all their stories, and all those families of instruments from different cultures were like friends to him, and he studied them and understood their workings and their histories. The old man is gone now, but he was my father. He told the stories to me, and now I will tell them to you.

This violin, or what we prefer to call a fiddle, began life many years ago with the felling of an old tree; well, actually several trees were brought together to make this instrument: cedar, maple, and ebony. All of these trees grew in different forests, and they were married by a man who knew their qualities and how to merge them to make a thing of beauty that was more than the sum of its parts . . . a small box with a sonorous voice, a violin, one of the most noble of humankind's creations.

This happened far from here, in another land. How did this fiddle come all the way here to reside in this dark shop among these strange musical folks? That is the story I will now tell you.

ABOUT THE AUTHOR

Stephen Cline has a bachelor's in literature and 20th century thought and expression and a master's in literature and rhetoric and composition, is a member of the Honor Society of Phi Kappa Phi, and is a recipient of an NEH Fellowship to study the Medieval sources of the Arthurian tales. He taught literature, creative writing, and composition for over twenty years, and has had numerous short stories, essays, and cartoons published in magazines and anthologies, including *Short Story, Surfer's Journal, Petroglyph, Easy Reader, Fretboard Journal, Surfer's Path* (UK), *H2O, Julian News, Lives On Board,* and *Inside English.* He also has been a guest lecturer at writing conferences in Washington and Hawaii.

Stephen's other novels are *Echoes Over Water, The Last Orange Grove,* and *The Queen's English.* He also is an accomplished musician and recording artist.

A fourth-generation Californian, Stephen now lives on the Big Island of Hawaii with his poet wife, Nancee.